U0051670

Ode to
the West Wind

EX-LIBRIS

©DEE TEN PUBLISHING CO

雪萊詩選／

西風頌

中英對照雙語版

Ode to
the West Wind

雪萊 —— 著

王明鳳 —— 譯

笛藤出版

　　唯美詩化的文字，猶如夜幕蒼穹中的密佈星羅，自悠久的歷史長河之中散發出璀璨迷人的耀目光環，是人類精神世界中無價的瑰寶。千百年來，由各種文字所組成的篇章，經由傳遞淬煉，使其在各種文學彙集而成的花園中不斷綻放出絢幻之花，讓人們沉浸於美好的閱讀時光。

　　作者們以凝練的語言、鮮明的節奏，反映著世界萬象的生活樣貌，並以各種形式向世人展現他們內心豐富多彩的情感世界。每個民族、地域的文化都有其精妙之處，西洋文學往往直接抒發作者的思想，愛、自由、和平，言盡而意亦盡，毫無造作之感。

　　18 ～ 19 世紀，西洋文學的發展進入彰顯浪漫主義色彩的時期。所謂浪漫主義，就是用熱情奔放的言辭、絢麗多彩的想像與直白誇張的表現手法，直接抒發出作者對理想世界熱切追求與渴望的情感。《世界經典文學 中英對照》系列，精選了浪漫主義時期一些作者們的代表作，包括泰戈爾的《新月集》、《漂鳥集》；雪萊的《西風頌》；濟慈的《夜鶯頌》；拜倫的《漫步在美的光影》；葉慈的《塵世玫瑰》。讓喜文之人盡情地徜徉於優美的字裡行間，領略作者及作品的無盡風采，享受藝術與美的洗禮。本系列所精選出的作品在世界文學領域中皆為經典名作，因此特別附上英文，方便讀者對照賞析英文詩意之美，並可同時提升英文閱讀與寫作素養。

在這一系列叢書當中，有對自然的禮讚，有對愛與和平的歌頌，有對孩童時代的讚美，也有對人生哲理的警示……，作者們在其一生中經歷了數次變革，以文字的形式寫下了無數天真、優美、現實、或悲哀的篇章，以無限的情懷吸引著所有各國藝文人士。文學界的名人郭沫若與冰心便是因受到了泰戈爾這位偉大的印度著名詩人所著詩歌的影響，在一段時期內寫出了很多類似的詩作。在世界文學界諸多名人當中有貴族、政治名人、社會名流、也有普羅大眾，他們來自不同的國家、種族，無論一生平順或是坎坷，但其所創作品無一不是充滿了對世間的熱愛，對未來美好世界的無限嚮往。

編按：由於經過時間變遷、地域上的區別，許多遣辭用句也多所改變，為期望能更貼近現代讀者，特將原譯文經過潤飾，希望讀者能以更貼近生活的語詞，欣賞雪萊所欲傳達的詩意哲理。

目 錄 /

西風頌。

Ode to the West Wind

懺悔／

走吧！月光下的荒原如此幽暗，

流雲已飲盡了傍晚最後的昏黃餘暉，

走吧！群聚的晚風很快地將召來黑暗；

天堂的靜謐之光將為深夜所遮掩。

不要逗留！時光消逝！一切都在高喊：走吧！

不要被那最後一滴淚珠所打動，那非出自柔情；

戀人的眼神如此黯淡冰冷，令人不敢奢求停駐。

本分和怠忽職守引領你回歸孤寂。

去吧，去吧！回到你那悲傷無聲的家中，

將痛苦的淚水灑落悲涼的爐旁，

看著幽靈般的暗影來回遊蕩，

將滿佈愁緒的強顏歡笑編織為奇異之網。

Remorse

AWAY! the moor is dark beneath the moon,

Rapid clouds have drunk the last pale beam of even:

Away! the gathering winds will call the darkness soon,

And profoundest midnight shroud the serene lights of heaven.

Pause not! the time is past! Every voice cries, Away!

Tempt not with one last tear thy friend's ungentle mood:

Thy lover's eye, so glazed and cold, dares not entreat thy stay:

Duty and dereliction guide thee back to solitude.

Away, away! to thy sad and silent home;

Pour bitter tears on its desolated hearth;

Watch the dim shades as like ghosts they go and come,

And complicate strange webs of melancholy mirth.

深秋的落葉將飄散在你的頭上，

春日的花露將閃爍在你的腳下：

你的心或世界必因死之霜降而凋零，

在子夜皺眉以及晨光微笑前夕，

內在的恬靜才得以交會。

愁雲在子夜安歇了，

疲倦的風沈寂下來，或者月色變得深沈，

不止息的海洋也知道要在狂暴中暫緩片刻；

一切的遷移、勞苦、悲傷都會適時止息。

墓中的你亦將安歇—然而，要等到幽靈，

從過往你所珍視的宅邸、庭園和荒野消散之際，

你的記憶、悔恨和沉思卻無法掙脫

兩人談論的音樂，以及那抹甜美微笑的光澤。

The leaves of wasted autumn woods shall float around thine head,

The blooms of dewy Spring shall gleam beneath thy feet:

But thy soul or this world must fade in the frost
that binds the dead,

Ere midnight's frown and morning's smile,
ere thou and peace, may meet.

The cloud shadows of midnight possess their own repose,

For the weary winds are silent, or the moon is in the deep;

Some respite to its turbulence unresting ocean knows;

Whatever moves or toils or grieves hath its appointed sleep.

Thou in the grave shalt rest:—yet, till the phantoms flee,

Which that house and heath and garden made dear
to thee erewhile,

Thy remembrance and repentance and deep musings are not free

From the music of two voices, and the light of one sweet smile.

無常／

我們有如遮蔽子夜月亮的雲朵；

不停地奔跑、閃耀和顫動，

在黑夜中綻放出燦爛的光芒！—但旋即

夜幕降臨之際瞬間迷失方向；

又像被遺忘的豎琴，不協調的弦聲，

每次彈奏都會發出不同的聲響，

那纖弱的樂器，每次重奏

都和上次的音調有所不同。

Mutability

We are as clouds that veil the midnight moon;

How restlessly they speed, and gleam, and quiver,

Streaking the darkness radiantly! —yet soon

Night closes round, and they are lost for ever;

Or like forgotten lyres, whose dissonant strings

Give various response to each varying blast,

To whose frail frame no second motion brings

One mood or modulation like the last.

我們睡下：一場夢能毒戕安息；

我們起身：游思又會玷污白晝；

我們感覺、思考、想像、哭笑，

不管是抱住悲傷，還是擺脫煩惱；

終究還是一樣！因為在世間，

一切的悲傷和喜悅都會溜走：

我們的明天不再像昨日，

除了「無常」，一切都會變幻。

We rest. —A dream has power to poison sleep;

We rise. —One wandering thought pollutes the day;

We feel, conceive or reason, laugh or weep;

Embrace fond woe, or cast our cares away:

It is the same! —For, be it joy or sorrow,

The path of its departure still is free:

Man's yesterday may ne'er be like his morrow;

Nought may endure but Mutability.

詠死亡／

在你所必去的陰間，沒有工作、沒有謀算、沒有知識、
更沒有智慧。

——《舊約・傳道書》

一個蒼白、冰冷、朦朧的笑容，

在星光寂寥的夜裡，如一顆流星

照耀著大海包圍的一座孤荒小島，

黎明的曙光還沒有發亮，

生命之火如此黯淡蒼白，

飄忽地劃過我們的腳邊，直到火光燃盡。

人類啊！請你鼓足靈魂的勇氣，

熬過世間的黑暗和風暴，

當波狀雲環繞之際，

沐浴在奇異之日的光芒中然後沉睡，

天堂和地獄將讓你得以自由，

得以進入命運的宇宙。

On Death

there is no work, nor device, nor knowledge, nor wisdom, in the grave, whither thou goest.

—Ecclesiastes

The pale, the cold, and the moony smile

Which the meteor beam of a starless night

Sheds on a lonely and sea-girt isle,

Ere the dawning of morn's undoubted light,

Is the flame of life so fickle and wan

That flits round our steps till their strength is gone.

O man! hold thee on in courage of soul

Through the stormy shades of thy wordly way,

And the billows of clouds that around thee roll

Shall sleep in the light of a wondrous day,

Where hell and heaven shall leave thee free

To the universe of destiny.

我們的感知滋生於現在，

我們的情感也在此萌生，

死亡是可怕的一擊，

讓未經過風浪的頭腦震驚：

想到我們的所知、所見、所感，

都將會消逝如不可解的謎題。

墳墓的另一頭藏著秘密，

除了我們的軀體，一切都在，

雖然這雙精細的眼睛和美妙的聽覺，

將再也無法存續、聆聽或觀看，

一切的偉大和神奇，

在這變幻的大千世界中。

有誰講述過無聲的死亡故事？

This world is the nurse of all we know,

This world is the mother of all we feel,

And the coming of death is a fearful blow

To a brain unencompass'd by nerves of steel:

When all that we know, or feel, or see,

Shall pass like an unreal mystery.

The secret things of the grave are there,

Where all but this frame must surely be,

Though the fine-wrought eye and the wondrous ear

No longer will live, to hear or to see

All that is great and all that is strange

In the boundless realm of unending change.

西風頌

有誰揭開過死亡背後的帷幕？

有誰到過彎曲開闊的墓穴？

將裡面的景象進行描述？

或者將現在的愛和恐懼

與未來的希望聯想在一起？

Who telleth a tale of unspeaking death?

Who lifteth the veil of what is to come?

Who painteth the shadows that are beneath

The wide-winding caves of the peopled tomb?

Or uniteth the hopes of what shall be

With the fears and the love for that which we see?

夏日黃昏的墓園／

晚風將淹沒落日餘韻的霧靄

吹散在遼闊的空中；

昏暗的傍晚將閃亮的金髮盤上，

深色的髮辮環繞著太陽倦怠的雙眼，

啊，無人喜歡的寂寥的黃昏，

正從那黑暗的山谷中徐徐爬來。

他們向那將逝的白日施咒，

影響了海洋、天空、星辰和大地；

光線、聲音、動作全都感受到強力的搖蕩，

因著神秘魔咒而有所感應。

風靜止了，或者那教堂頂上的枯草，

絲毫察覺不出風在飄動。

A Summer Evening Churchyard

THE wind has swept from the wide atmosphere

Each vapour that obscured the sunset's ray,

And pallid Evening twines its beaming hair

In duskier braids around the languid eyes of Day:

Silence and Twilight, unbeloved of men,

Creep hand in hand from yon obscurest glen.

They breathe their spells towards the departing day,

Encompassing the earth, air, stars, and sea;

Light, sound, and motion, own the potent sway,

Responding to the charm with its own mystery.

The winds are still, or the dry church-tower grass

Knows not their gentle motions as they pass.

雲朵，你亦如此。你那頂端

如火之金字塔在聖殿上聳立，

在靜默中服從神奇的咒語，

沐浴在天堂之光中，那模糊遙遠的塔尖，

逐漸消逝乃至不可見，

僅剩寂寥的星空凝聚成暮色。

死者在他們的石墓中安睡，

正在慢慢腐蝕；從蛆蟲的床底

發出若有似無的震顫聲，

一切生命都在黑暗裡振盪；

那聲波在肅穆中漸漸朦朧，

隱沒於幽暗和寂靜的空中。

Thou too, aerial pile, whose pinnacles

Point from one shrine like pyramids of fire,

Obey'st I in silence their sweet solemn spells,

Clothing in hues of heaven thy dim and distant spire,

Around whose lessening and invisible height

Gather among the stars the clouds of night.

The dead are sleeping in their sepulchres:

And, mouldering as they sleep, a thrilling sound,

Half sense half thought, among the darkness stirs,

Breathed from their wormy beds all living things around,

And, mingling with the still night and mute sky,

Its awful hush is felt inaudibly.

啊，美化了的死亡，就像這靜謐的夜晚，

這樣平靜、莊嚴，絲毫不令人畏懼：

我多希望，有如墓園中玩耍探尋的孩子那般，

看到死亡對肉眼隱瞞了甜美的秘密，

或是在他無聲無息的睡眠中，

永恆地保有美夢。

Thus solemnized and softened, death is mild

And terrorless as this serenest night.

Here could I hope, like some enquiring child

Sporting on graves, that death did hide from human sight

Sweet secrets, or beside its breathless sleep

That loveliest dreams perpetual watch did keep.

亞平寧山道／

聽啊，聽啊，我的瑪麗，

你聽亞平寧山正在低語，

它的話音落到屋頂上好似雷鳴，

又如北方岸邊

地牢裡的囚徒聽到的

狂瀾怒卷的一片海潮。

白天的亞平寧山

是巨大而灰暗的山嶺，

巍然屹立於天地之間；

但是在夜晚的星空下，

顯得幽暗、混沌、可怕，

彷彿會和風暴一起出發

籠罩一切……

Passage of the Apennines

Listen, listen, Mary mine,

To the whisper of the Apennine,

It bursts on the roof like the thunder's roar,

Or like the sea on a northern shore,

Heard in its raging ebb and flow

By the captives pent in the cave below.

The Apennine in the light of day

Is a mighty mountain dim and gray,

Which between the earth and sky doth lay,

But when night comes, a chaos dread

On the dim starlight then is spread,

And the Apennine walks abroad with the storm,

Shrouding...

往昔／

你是否會忘記那些我們沈醉

在愛情甜美亭榭之下的歡樂時光？

在屍體之上堆疊的是冰冷的

鮮花和樹葉，而非青苔。

鮮花是已逝的歡樂，

而葉子還殘存著希望。

忘懷逝者、忘卻過去了嗎？噢，然而

會有幽靈來為之復仇，

記憶會將心變成墳墓，

悔恨也會滑過憂鬱的心神，

可怖地對你耳語：

快樂一旦消失，便是痛苦。

The Past

Wilt thou forget the happy hours

Which we buried in Love's sweet bowers,

Heaping over their corpses cold

Blossoms and leaves, instead of mould?

Blossoms which were the joys that fell,

And leaves, the hopes that yet remain.

Forget the dead, the past? Oh, yet

There are ghosts that may take revenge for it,

Memories that make the heart a tomb,

Regrets which glide through the spirit's gloom,

And with ghastly whispers tell

That joy, once lost, is pain.

頌一朵凋零的紫羅蘭／

這朵花的香氣已經散失，

如你的吻對我吐露過的氣息；

這朵花的顏色已經褪去，

如你曾煥發過的明亮，只有你！

一個枯萎而僵死的形體，

在我悲涼的胸前茫然停留，

它以冷酷、沉默的安息，

折磨著我依然火熱的心。

我哭泣，但眼淚也不能讓它復生；

我嘆息，但再也沒有撲鼻的香氣；

這沉默順服的命運，

正是我所應得的。

On a Faded Violet

The odour from the flower is gone

Which like thy kisses breathed on me;

The colour from the flower is flown

Which glowed of thee and only thee!

A shrivelled, lifeless, vacant form,

It lies on my abandoned breast;

And mocks the heart, which yet is warm

With cold and silent rest.

I weep — my tears revive it not;

I sigh — it breathes no more on me:

Its mute and uncomplaining lot

Is such as mine should be.

召苦難／

來啊，快樂點！坐到我身邊，

在陰影下蒙著面紗的苦難：

有如嬌羞而閃躲的新娘，

在驕傲長袍下的悼詞，

將荒蕪予以神化！

來啊，快樂點！坐到我身邊，

在你看來，我好像很傷心，

我卻比你要快樂得多；

因為啊，姑娘，你的前額

正戴著悲傷的帽冠。

Invocation to Misery

Come, be happy! —sit near me,

Shadow-vested Misery:

Coy, unwilling, silent bride,

Mourning in thy robe of pride,

Desolation—deified!

Come, be happy! —sit near me:

Sad as I may seem to thee,

I am happier far than thou,

Lady, whose imperial brow

Is endiademed with woe.

我們早已如兄妹般

彼此親密熟悉；

我們共住在寂寞的屋中，

為期多年，而且

還要共度無數歲月。

這當然是惡運，

讓我們善加利用；

如果當愉悅消逝，而愛能存續，

我們就相愛吧！直到

心靈的地獄變成樂園。

來啊，快樂點！在此坐下吧

這片嫩草正供你休憩，

蟈蟈將在這裡快樂地

歌唱—在哀傷的世間

唯一的快樂！

Misery! we have known each other,

Like a sister and a brother

Living in the same lone home,

Many years—we must live some

Hours or ages yet to come.

Tis an evil lot, and yet

Let us make the best of it;

If love can live when pleasure dies,

We two will love, till in our eyes

This heart's Hell seem Paradise.

Come, be happy!—lie thee down

On the fresh grass newly mown,

Where the Grasshopper doth sing

Merrily—one joyous thing

In a world of sorrowing!

以垂柳做我們的帷帳，

讓你在我的臂彎中安睡；

曾經甜蜜的聲音和香氣，

已變得黯然，正好

我們可以鬱鬱沉睡。

哈！在你冰涼的血液中，

還跳躍著你不願承認的愛情，

你在低語—你在啜泣—

我火熱的心已經死了，

你冰冷的心是否在為我哀傷？

吻我吧，噢，你的唇是多麼冰冷！

你用雙臂環著我的脖頸—

它雖然柔軟，卻也冰冷死寂；

你的淚水滴落在我的臉上，

猶如被凝結的鉛所灼傷。

There our tent shall be the willow,

And mine arm shall be thy pillow;

Sounds and odours, sorrowful

Because they once were sweet, shall lull

Us to slumber, deep and dull.

Ha! thy frozen pulses flutter

With a love thou darest not utter.

Thou art murmuring—thou art weeping—

Is thine icy bosom leaping

While my burning heart lies sleeping?

Kiss me;—oh! thy lips are cold:

Round my neck thine arms enfold—

They are soft, but chill and dead;

And thy tears upon my head

Burn like points of frozen lead.

快到新婚的臥榻上來吧—

就設在墳墓的底下：

讓我們在黑暗中

埋葬愛情，再覆上寂滅—

我們將得以安息，沒有任何禁忌。

緊緊地摟著我，讓我們的心

像兩個影子合而為一，

直到這恐懼，

如消散的霧氣，

隱沒在永恆的夢中。

在長眠中，我們會夢到

自己從未哭泣；

結束生命的苦難啊，

就像歡笑夢中有你之際，

你夢見我正和她在一起。

Hasten to the bridal bed—

Underneath the grave 'tis spread:

In darkness may our love be hid,

Oblivion be our coverlid—

We may rest, and none forbid.

Clasp me till our hearts be grown

Like two shadows into one;

Till this dreadful transport may

Like a vapour fade away,

In the sleep that lasts alway.

We may dream, in that long sleep,

That we are not those who weep;

E'en as Pleasure dreams of thee,

Life-deserting Misery,

Thou mayst dream of her with me.

讓我們笑吧，對著

大地上的陰影歡笑，

就像狗兒對著月色下的雲朵吠叫，

就像在靜謐的深夜

不斷飄過的靈魂。

我們四周的廣大世界，

猶如許多木偶，

逢場作戲的舞臺，

這一切僅是徒勞，

我在哪裡？只不過是逢場作戲！

Let us laugh, and make our mirth,

At the shadows of the earth,

As dogs bay the moonlight clouds,

Which, like spectres wrapped in shrouds,

Pass o'er night in multitudes.

All the wide world, beside us,

Show like multitudinous

Puppets passing from a scene;

What but mockery can they mean,

Where I am—where thou hast been?

不要揭開這畫布／

不要揭開這張人稱

「生活」的畫布，它畫的不是真相，

不過是仿造我們所想的事物，

隨便在後面塗上顏料，掩藏著恐懼

和希望的雙重命運；無論是誰

在裂縫中編織著盲目和憂傷的幻影。

我知道曾經有人將它揭開過─他要尋找

迷失的心能予以寄託的溫柔愛情，

唉！他終究沒能找到！世上沒有這樣的

事物，能讓他稍稍心動。

於是，他在冷漠的人群中穿梭，

成為黑暗裡的光亮，像明亮的斑點

點綴在陰鬱的景色中，也像個追求真理的

精靈，卻發出和傳道者般的哀嘆。

Sonnet: Lift Not the
Painted Veil Which These Who Live

Lift not the painted veil which those who live

Call life: though unreal shapes be pictured there,

And it but mimic all we would believe

With colours idly spread,-behind, lurk Fear

And Hope, twin Destinies; who ever weave

Their shadows, o'er the chasm, sightless and drear.

I knew one who had lifted it-he sought,

For his lost heart was tender, things to love,

But found them not, alas! nor was there aught

The world contains, the which he could approve.

Through the unheeding many he did move,

A splendour among shadows, a bright blot

Upon this gloomy scene, a Spirit that strove

For truth, and like the Preacher, found it not.

印度小夜曲／

我從有你的夢中醒來，

那是午夜一場甜美的夢境，

晚風正輕輕地吹，

星星閃耀著光芒；

我從有你的夢中醒來，

我的腳邊有個精靈，

莫名所以地引領，

來到你的寢居窗前，親愛的！

悠揚的樂曲流淌在

暗夜中寂靜的水面—

金香木的芳香漸漸消散，

猶如夢境中的甜美想像；

夜鶯停止了抱怨，

將哀怨埋藏在心裡。

如同我必在你的懷中，

The Indian Serenade

I arise from dreams of thee

In the first sweet sleep of night,

When the winds are breathing low,

And the stars are shining bright

I arise from dreams of thee,

And a spirit in my feet

Hath led me—who knows how?

To thy chamber window, Sweet!

The wandering airs they faint

On the dark, the silent stream—

The champak odours fail

Like sweet thoughts in a dream;

The nightingale's complaint,

It dies upon her heart;

As I must on thine,

因為我所愛的是你！

啊，請將我從草坪上扶起！

我氣息奄奄，神志昏迷，衰竭無力！

你的愛如雨水吻在

我蒼白的唇和眼睫上。

我的臉龐如此白皙冰冷，

我的心在激烈地跳動；

啊，讓我的心緊握住你，

它終將會在那裡破碎。

Oh, beloved as thou art!

Oh lift me from the grass!

I die! I faint! I fail!

Let thy love in kisses rain

On my lips and eyelids pale.

My cheek is cold and white, alas!

My heart beats loud and fast;—

Oh! press it to thine own again,

Where it will break at last.

愛的哲學／

泉水總是匯入河流，

河流又匯入大海，

蒼穹中的微風混雜著

甜蜜的情感；

世上的所有都無獨有偶，

遵循著同一個神聖法則

彼此交融在一起，

為什麼我與你不能如是？

看那高山親吻著天空，

波濤也彼此相擁；

有誰見過花兒彼此不容，

如同兄弟間蔑視彼此？

陽光緊抱大地，

月光親吻海洋：

這些吻有什麼價值，

如果你我不能相吻？

Love's Philosophy

The fountains mingle with the river

And the rivers with the ocean,

The winds of heaven mix for ever

With a sweet emotion;

Nothing in the world is single,

All things by a law divine

In one another's being mingle—

Why not I with thine?

See the mountains kiss high heaven,

And the waves clasp one another;

No sister-flower would be forgiven

If it disdain'd its brother:

And the sunlight clasps the earth,

And the moonbeams kiss the sea—

What are all these kissings worth,

If thou kiss not me?

致雲雀／

為你喝采，快樂的精靈！

誰說你只是一隻鳥？

從天堂或那周圍，

傾注你的全心全意，

偶然間就能創造豐富的樂音。

你從地面一躍而起，

越飛越高，

似一團火雲，

在蔚藍天際中振翅，

不停地吟唱飛翔，飛翔吟唱。

金黃光輝緩緩現身

西沉的夕陽中。

穿梭於炫亮的彩雲，

你滑翔又旋而飛行，

猶如剛剛啟程的歡快，無拘無束。

To a Skylark

HAIL to thee, blithe spirit!

Bird thou never wert,

That from heaven or near it,

Pourest thy full heart

In profuse strains of unpremeditated art.

Higher still and higher

From the earth thou springest,

Like a cloud of fire;

The blue deep thou wingest,

And singing still dost soar, and soaring ever singest.

In the golden light'ning

Of the sunken sun,

O'er which clouds are bright'ning,

Thou dost float and run,

Like an unbodied joy whose race is just begun.

那淡紫微光

暈融於你的輕快飛翔；

恰如天空的星子

在白晝巨幕中，

無法窺見，卻能聽聞激昂的歡笑：

如同弓箭般銳利，

從銀白的天色迸出，

鋒利的光線，

在黎明晨光下愈加微弱，

無法窺見，卻能感覺它的存在。

大地和空氣，

充盈著你的高歌，

宛如靜謐的夜晚，

一片寂寥的雲朵，

流瀉出月的光華，滿溢天空。

The pale purple even

Melts around thy flight;

Like a star of heaven,

In the broad daylight

Thou art unseen, but yet I hear thy shrill delight—

Keen as are the arrows

Of that silver sphere

Whose intense lamp narrows

In the white dawn clear,

Until we hardly see, we feel that it is there.

All the earth and air

With thy voice is loud,

As when night is bare,

From one lonely cloud

The moon rains out her beams, and heaven is overflow'd.

我們不知道你是什麼；

什麼與你最為相仿？

從彩虹雲間流瀉出

的水珠固然晶亮，

卻不及你的旋律捎來的陣雨—

如同一位隱匿於

光明思想中的詩人，

唱著讚美的詩歌

直到世界被改造

充滿希望與同情，不再恐懼：

如同出身高貴的少女，

獨坐王宮塔樓，

抒發著她的愛情，

就在那幽靜的時刻，

甜蜜的音樂迴盪香閨；

What thou art we know not;

What is most like thee?

From rainbow clouds there flow not

Drops so bright to see,

As from thy presence showers a rain of melody:—

Like a poet hidden

In the light of thought,

Singing hymns unbidden,

Till the world is wrought

To sympathy with hopes and fears it heeded not:

Like a high-born maiden

In a palace tower,

Soothing her love-laden

Soul in secret hour

With music sweet as love, which overflows her bower;

如同閃爍金光的螢火蟲，

在凝結著露珠的山谷中，

在花草叢間，

到處可見輕盈的光，

花草遮擋了視線，使他不可得見：

如同隱蔽在綠葉中的

一朵玫瑰花，

和煦的風欲將花瓣吹散，

最終，濃郁的香氣

使得竊者沈醉其中。

春季的陣雨打在

晶瑩的草地發出的響聲，

花兒被雨滴喚醒，

這些被認為

快樂、清澈、鮮明的歌曲，都不及你的歌聲。

Like a glow-worm golden

 In a dell of dew,

  Scattering unbeholden

  Its aerial hue

Among the flowers and grass which screen it from the view:

 Like a rose embower'd

 In its own green leaves,

  By warm winds deflower'd,

  Till the scent it gives

Makes faint with too much sweet those heavy-wingèd thieves.

 Sound of vernal showers

 On the twinkling grass,

  Rain-awaken'd flowers—

  All that ever was

Joyous and clear and fresh—thy music doth surpass.

教教我們吧，精靈或是鳥兒，

你那甜蜜的思緒由何而來？

我從沒聽過

對愛情或對葡萄酒的讚譽，

能夠迸發出如你這般神聖的狂喜。

即使是婚禮上的合唱，

還是凱旋歸來的頌歌，

若是與你的歌聲相比，

僅存空洞的浮誇，

總有某處藏著些許缺憾。

你快樂的泉源

是由何而來？

是哪座原野、浪花或山峰？

是哪個天空或平原？

是你哪樣的愛情能無視於苦痛？

Teach us, sprite or bird,

What sweet thoughts are thine:

I have never heard

Praise of love or wine

That panted forth a flood of rapture so divine.

Chorus hymeneal,

Or triumphal chant,

Match'd with thine would be all

But an empty vaunt—

A thin wherein we feel there is some hidden want.

What objects are the fountains

Of thy happy strain?

What fields, or waves, or mountains?

What shapes of sky or plain?

What love of thine own kind? what ignorance of pain?

你的熱情明快，

令人不感疲倦，

煩惱的陰影

從未接近你，

你知道愛，但不懂得愛情滿溢的悲傷。

無論是安睡抑或清醒，

你看待死亡都比

我們凡人所能想像

更加地真實及深刻。

否則，你的曲調怎能如此透亮晶瑩？

我們總是瞻前顧後，

期待不存在的東西；

我們真摯的笑聲

也包含著苦澀，

那些能傾訴衷情的才是最甜美的歌。

With thy clear keen joyance

Languor cannot be:

Shadow of annoyance

Never came near thee:

Thou lovest, but ne'er knew love's sad satiety.

Waking or asleep,

Thou of death must deem

Things more true and deep

Than we mortals dream,

Or how could thy notes flow in such a crystal stream?

We look before and after,

And pine for what is not:

Our sincerest laughter

With some pain is fraught;

Our sweetest songs are those that tell of saddest thought.

如果我們可以擺脫

仇恨、驕傲和恐懼；

如果我們生來就不會

流淚和哭泣，

我們又怎麼能感覺到喜悅呢？

勝過種種愉悅的聲音

所具有的節拍，

勝過所有書中

所能發掘的珍寶，

超越詩人的技巧，還能蔑視腳下的大地！

只要我能學會你腦海中

二分之一的歡唱技巧；

那樣和諧的狂野，

就會自我的唇邊流瀉，

世界將認真傾聽我的聲音，如同我傾聽你的歌聲。

Yet, if we could scorn

Hate and pride and fear,

If we were things born

Not to shed a tear,

I know not how thy joy we ever should come near.

Better than all measures

Of delightful sound,

Better than all treasures

That in books are found,

Thy skill to poet were, thou scorner of the ground!

Teach me half the gladness

That thy brain must know;

Such harmonious madness

From my lips would flow,

The world should listen then, as I am listening now.

阿波羅禮讚／

在不成眠的時刻注視我躺下，

將繁星點綴的夜空當做帷帳，

在廣袤的月色下，

將夢境從我惺忪的睡眼前吹走─

當時間的母親─晨曦宣佈

夢境和月亮離去時，就將我喚醒。

我起身攀登那蔚藍的蒼穹，

沿著山峰和海面慢行，

將褪下的睡袍留在海面的泡沫上；

雲朵因我的步伐而變得火紅，山洞裡

充滿著我的光輝，而天空

也讓我擁抱綠色大地。

Hymn of Apollo

The sleepless Hours who watch me as I lie,

Curtained with star-inwoven tapestries

From the broad moonlight of the sky,

Fanning the busy dreams from my dim eyes,—

Waken me when their Mother, the gray Dawn,

Tells them that dreams and that the moon is gone.

Then I arise, and climbing Heaven's blue dome,

I walk over the mountains and the waves,

Leaving my robe upon the ocean foam;

My footsteps pave the clouds with fire; the caves

Are filled with my bright presence, and the air

Leaves the green earth to my embraces bare.

我用光線之劍，射殺了

欺騙，他喜歡夜晚而懼怕白日，

一切作惡或想作惡的人

都會遠離我，我的榮耀之光

讓善意與正義朝氣蓬勃，

直到夜晚開始統治，才被削弱。

我用大氣的色彩滋潤

雲朵、彩虹和花兒；

月球和繁星都在永恆的居所中

被我的能量所環繞；

天地之間任何燈盞發出的光亮，

終將合一，即是我所發出的光。

The sunbeams are my shafts, with which I kill

Deceit, that loves the night and fears the day;

All men who do or even imagine ill

Fly me, and from the glory of my ray

Good minds and open actions take new might,

Until diminished by the reign of night.

I feed the clouds, the rainbows, and the flowers

With their ethereal colours; the Moon's globe

And the pure stars in their eternal bowers

Are cinctured with my power as with a robe;

Whatever lamps on Earth or Heaven may shine

Are portions of one power, which is mine.

中午時分我在天空之巔佇立，

開始踱著不情願的腳步，

一步步走向大西洋的雲朵；

我的離開，讓雲朵啜泣皺眉。

我從西部的島嶼給他們安慰，

沒有什麼能比得上我燦爛的笑容。

我是宇宙的眼睛，它憑藉我

審視自己，辨出自己的神聖；

樂器和詩歌所發出的和諧之音，

所有的預言、醫藥、光明

自然或藝術的，都屬於我，

勝利及讚美，都屬於我。

I stand at noon upon the peak of Heaven,

Then with unwilling steps I wander down

Into the clouds of the Atlantic even;

For grief that I depart they weep and frown;

What look is more delightful than the smile

With which I soothe them from the western isle?

I am the eye with which the Universe

Beholds itself and knows itself divine;

All harmony of instrument or verse,

All prophecy, all medicine, is mine.

All light of Art or Nature;—to my song

Victory and praise in its own right belong.

秋：輓歌／

太陽不再溫暖，秋風淒號，

枯萎的樹木不斷嘆息，蒼白的花兒即將死去，

一年就要結束，

躺在她即將死去的大地上，穿上落葉織成的壽衣

一年就要告終。

來吧，出來吧，月份，

十一月到五月，

換上了悲傷的服裝

憑悼冷冰冰將死的一年，

又如飄忽的幽靈守護在她的墓場。

Autumn: A Dirge

The warm sun is falling, the bleak wind is wailing,

The bare boughs are sighing, the pale flowers are dying,

And the Year

On the earth is her death-bed, in a shroud of leaves dead,

Is lying.

Come, Months, come away,

From November to May,

In your saddest array;

Follow the bier

Of the dead cold Year,

And like dim shadows watch by her sepulchre.

淒涼的雨絲飄零，受凍的小蟲蠕動著，

充盈的河水、喪鐘般的雷聲隆隆，

都是為了即將逝去的一年；

歡快的燕子飛走，蜥蜴也躲進

洞穴之中。

來吧，出來吧，月份，

披上白色、黑色和灰色的衣衫，

讓輕快的姊妹們彈奏樂曲，

緊隨停屍架，

上面躺著那已逝的一年，

為她墓地上的青草，灑下滴滴淚水。

The chill rain is falling, the nipped worm is crawling,

The rivers are swelling, the thunder is knelling

For the Year;

The blithe swallows are flown, and the lizards each gone

To his dwelling.

Come, Months, come away;

Put on white, black and gray;

Let your light sisters play—

Ye, follow the bier

Of the dead cold Year,

And make her grave green with tear on tear.

月亮頌／

你的蒼白是否因為

攀登蒼穹及俯視大地帶來的疲憊，

獨自遊走

在與你出身不同的星辰之間，

所以你變幻無常，像憂傷的眼睛

遍尋不著值得效忠的目標？

The Moon

Art thou pale for weariness

Of climbing heaven and gazing on the earth,

Wandering companionless

Among the stars that have a different birth,

And ever changing, like a joyless eye

That finds no object worth its constancy?

詠夜／

迅速走過西方的波濤，

黑夜的精靈！

你從東邊雲霧繚繞的洞穴走出，

漫長寂寥的白晝之中，

你編織著快樂和恐懼的夢，

這讓你害怕又欣喜─

輕快地飛出來！

請披上一件灰色的斗篷，

繁星鑲嵌其中！

長髮遮住了白晝的雙眼，

親吻她吧，直到她疲倦，

漫步於城市、海洋和陸地，

讓一切都沉睡在你的魔杖下─

來吧，我長日的追求！

To Night

Swiftly walk over the western wave,

Spirit of Night!

Out of the misty eastern cave

Where, all the long and lone daylight,

Thou wovest dreams of joy and fear,

Which make thee terrible and dear, —

Swift be thy flight!

Wrap thy form in a mantle grey,

Star-inwrought!

Blind with thine hair the eyes of Day,

Kiss her until she be wearied out,

Then wander o'er city, and sea, and land,

Touching all with thine opiate wand—

Come, long-sought!

當我起身看到曙光，

我為你嘆息；

當太陽高升，露水消散，

全盛時期的正午躺在花叢樹梢間，

疲倦的白晝要去休息，

如同不受歡迎的賓客，

我為你嘆息。

你的胞弟「死亡」走來，哭喊道：

「你願意等我嗎？」

你的孩子「睡眠」，睡眼惺忪，

像正午的蜜蜂，嗡嗡道：

「我能靠在你身邊嗎？」

「你願意等我嗎？」

而我回答：「不，不是你！」

When I arose and saw the dawn,

I sighed for thee;

When light rode high, and the dew was gone,

And noon lay heavy on flower and tree,

And the weary Day turned to his rest,

Lingering like an unloved guest,

I sighed for thee.

Thy brother Death came, and cried

'Wouldst thou me?'

Thy sweet child Sleep, the filmy-eyed,

Murmured like a noontide bee

'Shall I nestle near thy side?

Wouldst thou me?' -And I replied

'No, not thee!'

死亡會降臨，

只是現在時候未到—

睡眠會在你逃離時來臨；

這兩者都不會讓我感到快樂

我只想要你，親愛的夜晚—

請你滑翔得快些吧，

快來，快來！

Death will come when thou art dead,

Soon, too soon -

Sleep will come when thou art fled;

Of neither would I ask the boon

I ask of thee, beloved Night -

Swift be thine approaching flight,

Come soon, soon!

宇宙流浪者／

告訴我，星星，你光亮的翅膀

讓你如燃燒般快速飛行，

在哪個黑夜的岩洞中

才得以束縛你的翅膀？

告訴我，月亮，你是這面色蒼白又灰頭土臉的

朝聖者，在往天堂的途中漂泊無家可歸，

在日或夜的哪個地方才能

讓你得以安歇？

疲倦的風啊，你漂泊不定，

像是被世界拋棄的過客

你是否仍在秘密的巢穴，

抑或樹林和波濤中棲身？

The World's Wanderers

Tell me, thou Star, whose wings of light

Speed thee in thy fiery flight,

In what cavern of the night

Will thy pinions close now?

Tell me, Moon, thou pale and grey

Pilgrim, of heaven's homeless way,

In what depth of night or day,

Seekest thou repose now?

Weary wind, who wanderest

Like the world's rejected guest,

Hast thou still some secret nest

On the tree or billow?

永逝的時光／

就像一位逝去老友的靈魂，

啊，永逝的時光。

一段旋律永遠飄零，

一顆心願消失無蹤

一場愛情無法永恆，

是你，永逝的時光。

曾有多少甜美的夢境，埋沒在

永逝的時光中；

無論憂傷抑或歡欣：

總是向前擲下一抹幻影，

多希冀他恆久留存—

在永逝的時光中。

Time Long Past

Like the ghost of a dear friend dead

Is Time long past.

A tone which is now forever fled,

A hope which is now forever past,

A love so sweet it could not last,

Was Time long past.

There were sweet dreams in the night

Of Time long past:

And, was it sadness or delight,

Each day a shadow onward cast

Which made us wish it yet might last—

That Time long past.

曾經惋惜、悔恨，

為那永逝的時光。

就像一位父親凝視著

愛子的屍身，直到永恆，

美麗如同記憶，在心頭迴盪，

迴盪在那永逝的時光。

There is regret, almost remorse,

For Time long past.

'Tis like a child's belovèd corse

A father watches, till at last

Beauty is like remembrance, cast

From Time long past.

歌曲／

你極少，極少現身，

愉悅的精靈！

為何你留下這許多

日日夜夜？

你已經逃離，

這乏味的日夜！

像我這樣謙卑之人如何

將你再次喚回？

伴隨著痛苦和嘲笑。

虛偽的精靈！你忘記了

那些你不需要的人。

Song

Rarely, rarely comest thou,

Spirit of Delight!

Wherefore hast thou left me now

Many a day and night?

Many a weary night and day

'Tis since thou art fled away.

How shall ever one like me

Win thee back again?

With the joyous and the free

Thou wilt scoff at pain.

Spirit false! thou hast forgot

All but those who need thee not.

有如蜥蜴見到了

晃動的葉影,

你悲傷且沮喪;

甚至連你哀傷的嘆息

也責備你不在附近,

但是你從不理會。

讓我將悲傷的小曲

譜成歡快的曲調,

你從不為憐憫而來,

你只為快樂而來;

屆時,將斬除

你那殘忍的翅膀,好將你留下。

As a lizard with the shade

Of a trembling leaf,

Thou with sorrow art dismayed;

Even the sighs of grief

Reproach thee, that thou art not near,

And reproach thou wilt not her.

Let me set my mournful ditty

To a merry measure;—

Thou wilt never come for pity,

Thou wilt come for pleasure;

Pity then will cut away

Those cruel wings, and thou wilt stay.

我愛你所鍾愛的一切，

愉悅的精靈！

披上綠葉的大地

和星星閃爍的夜空；

在秋日的夜晚和清晨，

當金黃的霧氣初升之際。

我愛雪和各種形式的

晶瑩的冰霜；

我愛波浪，微風，暴風雨，

近乎自然的種種，

我都喜愛，只要

未曾沾染人類的苦難。

I love all that thou lovest,

Spirit of Delight!

The fresh Earth in new leaves dressed,

And the starry night;

Autumn evening, and the morn

When the golden mists are born.

I love snow, and all the forms

Of the radiant frost;

I love waves, and winds, and storms,

Everything almost

Which is Nature's, and may be

Untainted by man's misery.

我喜愛靜謐的孤獨，

這樣的社會

寧靜、明智、美好；

我們之間，

有什麼區別？但你卻擁有

我一直在追求，卻不曾擁有過的東西。

我愛愛情─雖然他的翅膀，

像光一樣可以逃離，

但是，所有的事物中，

精靈啊，我最愛的是你

你是愛情和生命！來吧，

讓我的心再次成為你的歸鄉！

I love tranquil solitude,

And such society

As is quiet, wise, and good;

Between thee and me

What difference? but thou dost possess

The things I seek, not love them less.

I love Love—though he has wings,

And like light can flee,

But above all other things,

Spirit, I love thee—

Thou art love and life! Oh come!

Make once more my heart thy home!

哀歌／

哦，世界！哦，時間！哦，生命！

我登上最後一階，

不禁為我曾立足的地方顫抖；

你們幾時能再光華鼎盛？

噢，永不再有，永不再有！

從白天到黑夜，

喜悅已飛往天外；

初春、盛夏和嚴冬在我的心上

堆滿了悲哀，但是那歡快，

噢，永不再有，永不再有！

A Lament

O World! O Life! O Time!

On whose last steps I climb,

Trembling at that where I had stood before;

When will return the glory of your prime?

No more - oh, never more!

Out of the day and night

A joy has taken flight;

Fresh spring, and summer, and winter hoar

Move my faint heart with grief, but with delight

No more - oh, never more!

記憶／

飛得比夏日還輕快，

快過了青春的愉悅，

快過了幸福的夜晚，

你來去匆匆，不做停歇：

像是沒有綠葉的大地，

像是不能入睡的深夜，

像是失去快樂的心靈，

我孤獨地離開。

燕子在夏季還會再來，

有夜鶯的夜幕還會降臨—

但年輕的野天鵝願與

虛無的你同飛。

Remembrance

Swifter far than summer's flight,

Swifter far than youth's delight,

Swifter far than happy night,

Art thou come and gone:

As the earth when leaves are dead,

As the night when sleep is sped,

As the heart when joy is fled,

I am left lone, alone.

The swallow summer comes again,

The owlet night resumes her reign,

But the wild swan youth is fain

To fly with thee, false as thou.

我的心盼望每個清晨，

睡眠被憂傷取代，

即使我在冬天能借到

一絲春光，也是枉然。

如果百合要送給新娘，

玫瑰要戴在婦人頭上，

紫羅蘭是為了哀悼

少女的死亡；

那麼，就在我活著的

屍體上灑滿紫荊，

不要讓親愛的朋友

對我有任何的恐懼或希望。

My heart each day desires the morrow;

Sleep itself is turned to sorrow;

Vainly would my winter borrow

Sunny leaves from any bough.

Lilies for a bridal bed,

Roses for a matron's head,

Violets for a maiden dead;

Pansies let my flowers be:

On the living grave I bear

Scatter them without a tear,

Let no friend, however dear,

Waste one hope, one fear, for me.

音樂／

我渴望神聖的音樂，

我的心已飢渴得如枯萎的花瓣；

讓瓊漿般的旋律傾灑而下吧，

讓銀色雨滴般的音樂灑下吧；

像沒有甘露的草原，等待細雨，

我喘息、暈眩，等待被音樂喚醒；

我要啜飲那瓊漿玉液般的美聲，

來吧，來吧，我已渴求不已；

音樂解放了盤據我心頭的毒蛇，

憂慮跳上心頭試圖讓蛇窒息，

這優美的曲調，透過每條血脈

流進了我的心靈和腦海。

Music

I pant for the music which is divine,

My heart in its thirst is a dying flower;

Pour forth the sound like enchanted wine,

Loosen the notes in a silver shower;

Like a herbless plain, for the gentle rain,

I gasp, I faint, till they wake again.

Let me drink of the spirit of that sweet sound,

More, oh more,—I am thirsting yet;

It loosens the serpent which care has bound

Upon my heart to stifle it;

The dissolving strain, through every vein,

Passes into my heart and brain.

就像一朵乾枯的紫羅蘭，

在銀色的湖邊成長，

驕陽將盛滿雨露的杯子飲盡，

霧靄也無法讓它解渴—

花兒就這樣死去，仍殘存芳香

搧動著風的翅膀，在碧波上翱翔—

就像一個人正在啜飲金杯中

那閃耀著泡沫光彩的瓊漿，

因為魔女在杯沿上留下了

神聖的吻痕，等他來享受……

As the scent of a violet withered up,

Which grew by the brink of a silver lake,

When the hot noon has drained its dewy cup,

And mist there was none its thirst to slake—

And the violet lay dead while the odour flew

On the wings of the wind o'er the waters blue—

As one who drinks from a charmed cup

Of foaming, and sparkling, and murmuring wine,

Whom, a mighty Enchantress filling up,

Invites to love with her kiss divine...

當一盞燈被打碎了／

當一盞燈被打碎了，

光芒就會在塵囂中覆滅；

當雲朵在空中散去，

彩虹的光輝也隨之消逝。

若是琴斷了弦，

悠揚的曲調就會變得沉寂；

若將話語一次訴盡，

很快就會忘卻愛情的甜蜜。

就像樂音和光明必然與燈盞、詩琴相伴，

倘若精神已然消沉，

心靈就無法奏出美妙和弦：

沒有歌聲，只有哀號，

像是從荒墟一隅吹來的風，

像是悲哀號叫的波濤，

為已逝的水手敲響喪鐘。

When the Lamp Is Shattered

When the lamp is shattered

The light in the dust lies dead—

When the cloud is scattered,

The rainbow's glory is shed.

When the lute is broken,

Sweet tones are remembered not;

When the lips have spoken,

Loved accents are soon forgot.

As music and splendour

Survive not the lamp and the lute,

The heart's echoes render

No song when the spirit is mute—

No song but sad dirges,

Like the wind through a ruined cell,

Or the mournful surges

That ring the dead seaman's knell.

只要兩顆心結合，

愛情立刻會飛離精美的巢，

其中弱小的一方

肯定有過煎熬。

啊，愛情！你在哀傷

世事無常，

為什麼非要找那脆弱的心靈

作為搖籃、住所和墓場？

你被熱情顛簸，

就像飛鳥因風暴而飄搖；

你被理智嘲笑，

猶如冬日天空中那高掛的暖陽。

你巢中的橡木

將會腐朽，當寒風到來，

枯葉凋零，你豪華的房屋

就會讓你陷入嘲笑。

When hearts have once mingled,

Love first leaves the well-built nest;

The weak one is singled

To endure what it once possessed.

O Love! who bewailest

The frailty of all things here,

Why choose you the frailest

For your cradle, your home, and your bier?

Its passions will rock thee,

As the storms rock the ravens on high;

Bright reason will mock thee,

Like the sun from a wintry sky.

From thy nest every rafter

Will rot, and thine eagle home

Leave thee naked to laughter,

When leaves fall and cold winds come.

魔鬼的散步／

一天，魔鬼起了個大早，

開始精心地裝扮，

並穿上了節日的盛裝。

穿上靴子以隱蔽雙蹄，

戴上手套以遮掩魔爪，

並用帽子掩藏了頭上的犄角，

他瀟灑地走上了龐德街，

彷彿一位闊少。

他安穩坐在倫敦城裡，

在天空透出光亮前：

開始和一個親信的小鬼聊天，

談宗教、談醜聞，天南地北，

直到拂曉。

The Devil's Walk

Once, early in the morning, Beelzebub arose,

With care his sweet person adorning,

He put on his Sunday clothes.

He drew on a boot to hide his hoof,

He drew on a glove to hide his claw,

His horns were concealed by a Bras Chapeau,

And the Devil went forth as natty a Beau

As Bond-street ever saw.

He sate him down, in London town,

Before earth's morning ray;

With a favourite imp he began to chat,

On religion, and scandal, this and that,

Until the dawn of day.

接著他到了詹姆士廣場，

又走訪了聖保羅教堂，

他與每位聖徒都有好交情，

雖然他們守規矩，而他放蕩。

魔鬼是一個園藝師；

由於惡草總是長得最快，

我知道，當他環顧田園時，

心裡一定覺得舒暢。

他窺看每扇窗戶及每個圈場，

探看他肥美的牲畜，

他齜牙咧嘴地稱許牲畜，並露出自己的魔爪，

即使牲畜們樂於為他所用，

仍因懼怕魔鬼的醜陋而畏怯。

And then to St. James's Court he went,

And St. Paul's Church he took on his way;

He was mighty thick with every Saint,

Though they were formal and he was gay.

The Devil was an agriculturist,

And as bad weeds quickly grow,

In looking over his farm, I wist,

He wouldn't find cause for woe.

He peeped in each hole, to each chamber stole,

His promising live-stock to view;

Grinning applause, he just showed them his claws,

And they shrunk with affright from his ugly sight,

Whose work they delighted to do.

撒旦將他的紅鼻子伸進了窄縫，

也許你會認為，這有什麼呢？

那些可憐的綿羊！他們沒做什麼

只是在整理衣著，或是在安排舞會，

而魔鬼卻要窺伺一切。

這一位牧師，他祈禱時總有魔鬼

緊緊挨著坐在旁邊

他聲稱如果誘惑者魔鬼膽敢現身，

他絕不會讓魔鬼張狂。

哈！哈！老魔鬼尼克心想，這可真是老調重彈，

要是沒了我這親愛的魔鬼，

你連馬車都開不了。

Satan poked his red nose into crannies so small

One would think that the innocents fair,

Poor lambkins! were just doing nothing at all

But settling some dress or arranging some ball,

But the Devil saw deeper there.

A Priest, at whose elbow the Devil during prayer

Sate familiarly, side by side,

Declared that, if the Tempter were there,

His presence he would not abide.

Ah! ah! thought Old Nick, that's a very stale trick,

For without the Devil, O favourite of Evil,

In your carriage you would not ride.

接著撒旦又看到一位昏庸的國王，

他的王宮和自己的莊園同樣熱鬧，

有許多小鬼在四周飛行，

一會兒搖旗吶喊，一會兒扭動棘刺。

哈！哈！這裡真是座好牧場，

我的牲畜在這裡會長得比別處好；

在這他們吃的是血腥的新聞，

喝的是垂死者的呻吟，

他們不會空著肚子睡覺，

一定能吃得腦滿腸肥。

Satan next saw a brainless King,

Whose house was as hot as his own;

Many Imps in attendance were there on the wing,

They flapped the pennon and twisted the sting,

Close by the very Throne.

Ah! ah! thought Satan, the pasture is good,

My Cattle will here thrive better than others;

They dine on news of human blood,

They sup on the groans of the dying and dead,

And supperless never will go to bed;

Which will make them fat as their brothers.

他的牲畜像那些嗜血的同伴一樣

新鮮溫熱的血水來自西班牙的田野

在那裡用毀滅來犁出一條血路，

嫩芽剛探出來就被大地凍僵；

在那裡地獄是勝利的犧牲品，

榮耀是陣亡士兵獲得的回報。

肥得有如愛爾蘭岸邊的惡鳥

用鮮血滿足貪欲

環繞著卡斯雷輕快地飛翔，

掠奪愛國者血淋淋的心臟

從寡婦發狂似緊抱的懷中大肆掠奪，

然後在天明之前離去

Fat as the Fiends that feed on blood,

Fresh and warm from the fields of Spain,

Where Ruin ploughs her gory way,

Where the shoots of earth are nipped in the bud,

Where Hell is the Victor's prey,

Its glory the meed of the slain.

Fat—as the Death-birds on Erin's shore,

That glutted themselves in her dearest gore,

And flitted round Castlereagh,

When they snatched the Patriot's heart, that HIS grasp

Had torn from its widow's maniac clasp,

—And fled at the dawn of day.

肥得像墳墓中的屍蟲，

在腐朽中盡情地歡騰

在黑暗中度日，

緩慢匍匐而行

肥得像貴族感情用事的大腦：

被鑲金的玩具寵壞了，

厭倦的時候，就把糖果送人，

一會又哭著討糖吃，像鬧脾氣的孩子。

由於太胖了，他的背心

在君主接見前，無論怎樣拉緊，

也扣不上肚子上的鈕扣；

他把馬褲穿得像兩輪半月，

突出在他肥厚的雙臀上。

Fat—as the Reptiles of the tomb,

That riot in corruption's spoil,

That fret their little hour in gloom,

And creep, and live the while.

Fat as that Prince's maudlin brain,

Which, addled by some gilded toy,

Tired, gives his sweetmeat, and again

Cries for it, like a humoured boy.

For he is fat,—his waistcoat gay,

When strained upon a levee day,

Scarce meets across his princely paunch;

And pantaloons are like half-moons

Upon each brawny haunch.

在他那空虛的頭顱和心中，

竟然能裝這麼多的牛肉！

足以讓二十個人吃飽，

還能把馬褲撐出裂痕。

哈，哈！有時候魔鬼也被稱為「自然法則」

能充分滿足權貴人士，

讓他們的容貌和舉止

能和先祖十分相像。

撒旦見到律師殺害了一條毒蛇，

因為蛇要爬到他的餐桌上，

撒旦想到，這是多麼不可思議，就像

該隱怒殺亞伯一樣。

How vast his stock of calf! when plenty

Had filled his empty head and heart,

Enough to satiate foplings twenty,

Could make his pantaloon seams start.

The Devil (who sometimes is called Nature),

For men of power provides thus well,

Whilst every change and every feature,

Their great original can tell.

Satan saw a lawyer a viper slay,

That crawled up the leg of his table,

It reminded him most marvellously

Of the story of Cain and Abel.

當一位富裕地主

在富饒的田野裡踱步，

看著他健壯的牲畜，

盤算著有多少收入的時候，忍不住輕哼小曲；

魔鬼就漫遊在這樣的人間，

並哼唱著來自地獄的歌。

是啊，他要是全身血腥，

情願做撒旦忠心的奴僕；

他們藉由掠奪而更為富有

搶走窮人的麵包，

將流浪者所有的家當

堆集成富人的奢華。

The wealthy yeoman, as he wanders

His fertile fields among,

And on his thriving cattle ponders,

Counts his sure gains, and hums a song;

Thus did the Devil, through earth walking,

Hum low a hellish song.

For they thrive well whose garb of gore

Is Satan's choicest livery,

And they thrive well who from the poor

Have snatched the bread of penury,

And heap the houseless wanderer's store

On the rank pile of luxury.

主教雖腦滿腸肥，但飛黃騰達；

律師雖弱不禁風，也飛黃騰達，

因為在他們的教袍和假髮底下，

都隱藏在著來自地獄的生機。

然而豬玀總被認為是不潔的，

哪怕他們吃的是最高等的糧草；

鸕鶿即使日夜不停地進食，

也如同犯罪般地瘦弱。

噢，是什麼讓這地獄之父

笑得合不攏嘴？

他為何愉悅地脫下衣物

蹦蹦跳跳、歡欣鼓舞，還揮動雙翼，

側身而行、斜睨橫目，還旋轉棘刺

並膽敢現出他的原形？

The Bishops thrive, though they are big;

The Lawyers thrive, though they are thin;

For every gown, and every wig,

Hides the safe thrift of Hell within.

Thus pigs were never counted clean,

Although they dine on finest corn;

And cormorants are sin-like lean,

Although they eat from night to morn.

Oh! why is the Father of Hell in such glee,

As he grins from ear to ear?

Why does he doff his clothes joyfully,

As he skips, and prances, and flaps his wing,

As he sidles, leers, and twirls his sting,

And dares, as he is, to appear?

因為一個政治家獨自朝向他走來，

只有面對他，魔鬼才敢將

自己的一切都展露出來。

因為他們的情誼永遠堅固。

剛看到這個熟悉的歡迎信號，

戒備中的妖魔們尋找他們的君王，

從那斯蒂吉亞的冥幽裡

立即飛向他們的魔王。

慘白的忠誠，他那滿是罪疚的額上

穿戴著血腥的帽冠

地獄之犬：殺戮、貧苦、災難

永不饜足，一擁而上；

魔鬼在西班牙曾予以餵食

用人類的鮮血和傷悲！

A statesman passed—alone to him,

The Devil dare his whole shape uncover,

To show each feature, every limb,

Secure of an unchanging lover.

At this known sign, a welcome sight,

The watchful demons sought their King,

And every Fiend of the Stygian night,

Was in an instant on the wing.

Pale Loyalty, his guilt-steeled brow,

With wreaths of gory laurel crowned:

The hell-hounds, Murder, Want and Woe,

Forever hungering, flocked around;

From Spain had Satan sought their food,

'Twas human woe and human blood!

聽啊！那是大地震動的聲音，

國王們驚慌了，侵略者顫抖了，

惡徒們被嚇得鴉雀無聲，

因為，他們的撒旦突然消失了。

今天，魔鬼們歡快地聚會，

慶祝他們的首領回來，

他們高興地看到地獄之王

已將地獄的圍欄焚毀。

但是，魔鬼的目光

如理智之眼那般銳利，

地獄之王啊，我認為

沒什麼可慶祝。

Hark! the earthquake's crash I hear,—

Kings turn pale, and Conquerors start,

Ruffians tremble in their fear,

For their Satan doth depart.

This day Fiends give to revelry

To celebrate their King's return,

And with delight its Sire to see

Hell's adamantine limits burn.

But were the Devil's sight as keen

As Reason's penetrating eye,

His sulphurous Majesty I ween,

Would find but little cause for joy.

因為理智之子已經看清，

不等命運走到盡頭，

就會讓暴君的面孔

像他懦弱的靈魂一樣僵死。

For the sons of Reason see

That, ere fate consume the Pole,

The false Tyrant's cheek shall be

Bloodless as his coward soul.

時間╱

深不可測的大海啊！歲月就是你的波瀾；

時間的海洋啊，滿是深沉的悲戚，

鹹味竟是來自於人類的淚滴！

你的波濤浩渺無岸，水面上

潮汐交替，那就是人生的界邊！

雖然你已不屑於捕食，卻依然不斷地咆哮，

將那破碎的船隻無情地吐在岸邊；

你平靜時陰險，洶湧時猙獰，

啊，有誰敢在變幻莫測的海面

駕著小船航行？

Time

Unfathomable Sea! whose waves are years,

Ocean of Time, whose waters of deep woe

Are brackish with the salt of human tears!

Thou shoreless flood, which in thy ebb and flow

Claspest the limits of mortality!

And sick of prey, yet howling on for more,

Vomitest thy wrecks on its inhospitable shore;

Treacherous in calm, and terrible in storm,

Who shall put forth on thee,

Unfathomable Sea?

一個共和主義者有感於波拿巴的垮台／

我恨你啊，垮台的暴君！當我

想到像你這樣苟延殘喘的奴隸，

竟然也能在自由的墳墓上跳舞狂歡，

就感到無限傷感。你本可以

穩坐在寶座上直到如今，可你選擇了

滿是脆弱和血腥的輝煌，最終還是

被時間毀滅在寂靜裡。我寧願殺戮、背叛

奴役、貪婪、恐懼和邪念與你相伴入夢，

並讓它們的使者將你窒息。唉，可惜

我知道為時已晚，因為你和法蘭西一起

化為了塵土：原來美德還有一個比暴力和欺騙

更可惡的敵人：那就是古老的習慣，

這種罪惡是合法的；還有由時間塑造的那個

血腥形象，那最邪惡的信念。

Feelings of a Republican on the Fall of Bonaparte

I hated thee, fallen Tyrant! I did groan

To think that a most unambitious slave,

Like thou, should dance and revel on the grave

Of Liberty. Thou mightst have built thy throne

Where it had stood even now: thou didst prefer

A frail and bloody pomp, which Time has swept

In fragments towards oblivion. Massacre,

For this, I prayed, would on thy sleep have crept,

Treason and Slavery, Rapine, Fear, and Lust,

And stifled thee their minister. I know

Too late, since thou and France are in the dust,

That Virtue owns a more eternal foe

Than Force or Fraud: old Custom, legal Crime,

And bloody Faith, and foulest birth of Time.

1819 年的英格蘭／

一位老邁、瘋狂、盲目、可鄙，且垂死的國王—

昏庸的王子們像渣滓，遭受著

公眾的蔑視，是從泥濘裡挖出的泥漿—

統治者們既看不見，感覺不到，永遠也不會知道，

他們僅僅會像水蛭一樣吸附著垂死的國家，

直到他們被鮮血沖昏，不戰而敗—

人民在荒蕪的田中挨餓，遭受殺戮—

軍隊由於破壞了自由，已經

成為一把雙刃劍，對誰都揮舞著刀刃；

神聖而充滿希望的法律，其實是害人的陷阱；

失去基督和上帝的宗教，只是一本被封閉的書；

一座參議院，在那裡史上最惡劣的法令猶未廢除—

啊，也許會從一片墳墓裡，出現一個光輝的

幻影，照亮我們動盪不安的日子。

England in 1819

An old, mad, blind, despised, and dying king, —

Princes, the dregs of their dull race, who flow

Through public scorn, —mud from a muddy spring, —

Rulers who neither see, nor feel, nor know,

But leech like to their fainting country cling,

Till they drop, blind in blood, without a blow, —

A people starved and stabbed in the untilled field, —

An army, which liberticide and prey

Makes as a two-edged sword to all who wield, —

Golden and sanguine laws which tempt and slay;

Religion Christless, Godless -a book sealed;

A Senate, —Time's worst statute unrepealed,—

Are graves from which a glorious Phantom may

Burst, to illumine our tempestuous day.

西風頌／

1

狂暴的西風啊，生命之秋的呼吸

你雖無形，但枯葉已被你橫掃，

就像魔鬼見到了巫師，匆匆躲避：

黃的、黑的、灰的，紅得像是患上熱病，

落葉有如得到傳染病般變色：噢，西風，

是你駕車將帶翅的種子送到

黑暗的床上，它們在冰冷幽深處安眠，

如同墓穴中的死屍般，直到

你的春天姊姊在晴空中，

吹起她的號角，響徹沉睡的大地

（吹醒嫩芽，像餵飽空中的羊群）

平原和山峰上充滿著色彩和芳香：

Ode to the West Wind

1

O WILD West Wind, thou breath of Autumn's being

Thou from whose unseen presence the leaves dead

Are driven, like ghosts from an enchanter fleeing,

Yellow, and black, and pale, and hectic red,

Pestilence-stricken multitudes! O thou

Who chariotest to their dark wintry bed

The winged seeds, where they lie cold and low,

Each like a corpse within its grave, until

Thine azure sister of the Spring shall blow

Her clarion o'er the dreaming earth, and fill

(Driving sweet buds like flocks to feed in air)

With living hues and odours plain and hill;

放蕩不羈的精靈啊，你無所不在；

既保護又破壞；聽吧，聽吧！

2

當空中一片混沌，淹沒在你的急流中時，

浮雲就像大地上的落葉被撕扯得

遠離了天空和海洋的糾纏，

成了雨和電的使者，飄灑在

你磅礡大氣的湛藍海面，

就像甩動著一頭閃耀的長髮，

從遙遠而模糊的天邊，

到九霄的雲天，風雨欲來的捲髮在

四處飄搖。對即將逝去的一年，

Wild Spirit, which art moving everywhere;

Destroyer and preserver; hear, O hear!

2

Thou on whose stream, mid the steep sky's commotion,

Loose clouds like earth's decaying leaves are shed,

Shook from the tangled boughs of heaven and ocean,

Angels of rain and lightning! there are spread

On the blue surface of thine airy surge,

Like the bright hair uplifted from the head

Of some fierce Maenad, even from the dim verge

Of the horizon to the zenith's height,

The locks of the approaching storm. Thou dirge

你唱著哀歌，這幽靜的黑夜，

將成為這廣闊墓場的圓頂，

你無窮的力量正在裡面凝聚；

那是你的渾然之氣，可以迸發出

黑色的雨水、冰雹和火焰：你聽啊！

3

是你將藍色地中海從夏日夢境中喚醒，

清澈迴旋的水流

將它催眠入夢；

在巴亞海灣的一座浮石島邊，

它夢到古老的宮殿和樓閣

在粼粼水波裡震顫流動，

Of the dying year, to which this closing night

Will be the dome of a vast sepulchre,

Vaulted with all thy congregated might

Of vapours, from whose solid atmosphere

Black rain, and fire, and hail, will burst: O hear!

3

Thou who didst waken from his summer dreams

The blue Mediterranean, where he lay,

Lull'd by the coil of his cryst a lline streams,

Beside a pumice isle in Baiae's bay,

And saw in sleep old palaces and towers

Quivering within the wave's intenser day,

到處長滿了青苔，開遍了野花，

芳香得令人沉醉！為了讓路給你，

大西洋裡洶湧的波濤

劈裂為峽谷，海峽深處的

水中花朵及爛泥中的樹木

覆蓋著了無生氣的枯葉，一聽到

你的聲音，立刻被嚇得臉色發青：

顫抖著、畏縮著：你聽啊！

4

如果我是一片被你吹起的落葉，

如果我是和你一同遨遊的雲朵，

如果我是能在你的威力下呼吸的

波浪，能共享你心跳的力量，也絕不會

像你那樣的自由，無拘無束！

如果我能像在少年時，隨風起舞

All overgrown with azure moss, and flowers

So sweet, the sense faints picturing them! Thou

For whose path the Atlantic's level powers

Cleave themselves into chasms, while far below

The sea-blooms and the oozy woods which wear

The sapless foliage of the ocean, know

Thy voice, and suddenly grow gray with fear,

And tremble and despoil themselves: O hear!

4

If I were a dead leaf thou mightest bear;

If I were a swift cloud to fly with thee;

A wave to pant beneath thy power, and share

The impulse of thy strength, only less free

Than thou, O uncontrollable! if even

I were as in my boyhood, and could be

作為你的旅伴，在空中悠遊

因為，當時想和你一起飛到雲霄

並不只是夢境，我今天就不會

這樣焦急地為你祈禱。

啊，把我當做水波、落葉和浮雲，高高舉起吧，

我在生活的荊棘中摔倒，淌著血！

被歲月重壓、征服的生命啊，

原來你和我一樣桀驁不馴。

5

讓我成為你的豎琴吧，即使像森林一樣：

終將落葉飄散零落大地又何妨！

我所能演奏的巨大聲響

The comrade of thy wanderings over heaven,

As then, when to outstrip thy skiey speed

Scarce seem'd a vision—I would ne'er have striven

As thus with thee in prayer in my sore need.

O! lift me as a wave, a leaf, a cloud!

I fall upon the thorns of life! I bleed!

A heavy weight of hours has chain'd and bow'd

One too like thee—tameless, and swift, and proud.

5

Make me thy lyre, even as the forest is:

What if my leaves are falling like its own!

The tumult of thy mighty harmonies

能讓人感受到濃濃的秋意：

雖有哀傷也有甜蜜。啊，希望你給了我

狂熱的精神！勇士啊，讓我們合一！

請將我那枯竭的思緒吹落在世間，

讓它如落葉般化為新的生命！

啊，請聆聽這首咒語般的詩篇，

將我的言語，如灰燼和火星一般

從尚未熄滅的爐中灑向人間！

透過我的嘴唇讓沉睡的大地

大聲宣告預言！西風啊，

如果冬天來了，春天還會遠嗎？

Will take from both a deep autumnal tone,

Sweet though in sadness. Be thou, Spirit fierce,

My spirit! Be thou me, impetuous one!

Drive my dead thoughts over the universe,

Like wither'd leaves, to quicken a new birth;

And, by the incantation of this verse,

Scatter, as from an unextinguish'd hearth

Ashes and sparks, my words among mankind!

Be through my lips to unawaken'd earth

The trumpet of a prophecy! O Wind,

If Winter comes, can Spring be far behind?

奧西曼德斯／

我遇見一位來自古老國家的遊客，

他說：那兩座底部已經折斷的巨大石像

在沙漠中屹立著……旁邊的沙堆中，

還埋著半邊破碎的面部石像：眉頭微蹙，

嘴唇乾癟，威嚴的面孔中透著輕蔑，

充分說明了雕刻家的技巧栩栩如生，

在無生命的岩石上仍刻劃出激情，

雖然雕刻之手不在，初衷亦不復返。

石像基座上還刻著：

「我是奧西曼德斯，王中之王。

強悍的人，有誰能與我的功績相比！」

這裡就是一切，別無其他。

在無邊無際的荒墟周圍，

只見一片荒涼而寂寥的沙漠。

Ozymandias

I met a traveler from an antique land

Who said: Two vast and trunkless legs of stone

Stand in the desert... Near them, on the sand,

Half sunk, a shattered visage lies, whose frown,

And wrinkled lip, and sneer of cold command

Tell that its sculptor well those passions read

Which yet survive, stamped on these lifeless things,

The hand that mocked them, and the heart that fed.

And on the pedestal these words appear:

"My name is Ozymandias, king of kings:

Look on my works, ye Mighty, and despair!"

Nothing beside remains. Round the decay

Of that colossal wreck, boundless and bare

The lone and level sands stretch far away.

愛爾蘭人之歌／

即使繁星消散，光明的泉源

陷入無際的混沌和黑暗中，

大廈坍塌，田園也被掠奪，

但是，愛爾蘭啊，你絕不能失去勇氣！

看哪！四周都是殘垣斷壁，

我們的祖宅已傾頹，

只有得勝的敵人馳騁於土地上，

我們的戰士卻已在沙場中犧牲。

啊，曾經帶來歡愉的豎琴已破碎，

啊，家鄉輕快的歌曲也變得沉默；

只傳來了戰歌，彷彿戰場上的

廝殺聲和劍戟碰撞聲在耳旁迴響。

The Irishman's Song

The stars may dissolve, and the fountain of light

May sink into ne'er ending chaos and night,

Our mansions must fall, and earth vanish away,

But thy courage, O Erin! may never decay.

See! the wide wasting ruin extends all around,

Our ancestors' dwellings lie sunk on the ground,

Our foes ride in triumph throughout our domains,

And our mightiest heroes lie stretched on the plains.

Ah! dead is the harp which was wont to give pleasure,

Ah! sunk is our sweet country's rapturous measure,

But the war note is waked, and the clangour of spears,

The dread yell of Sloghan yet sounds in our ears.

啊！英雄們到哪去了？他們死得壯烈，

他們倒下，任鮮血流淌在荒漠中，

他們化身鬼魂，號叫聲伴著暴風，

不斷地號召：「同胞們，復仇啊！」

Ah! where are the heroes! triumphant in death,

Convulsed they recline on the blood-sprinkled heath,

Or the yelling ghosts ride on the blast that sweeps by,

And my countrymen! vengeance! incessantly cry.

我們別時和見時不同／

我們的別時和見時不同，

心事重重，但表露不盡，

我的心頭沈重壓抑，

你卻對我充滿懷疑——

歡樂就在一瞬散盡。

那個時刻永遠消逝了，

像閃電才出現就轉眼消失——

像雪花般落水即融——

又像陽光照射在潮水上，

旋即就被陰影埋葬。

We Meet Not As We Parted

We meet not as we parted,

We feel more than all may see;

My bosom is heavy-hearted,

And thine full of doubt for me: —

One moment has bound the free.

That moment is gone for ever,

Like lightning that flashed and died —

Like a snowflake upon the river —

Like a sunbeam upon the tide,

Which the dark shadows hide.

那歲月中的一瞬間，

變成生活苦痛的源頭；

愉悅的瓊漿立刻變得苦澀—

再美的幻景也不能長久！

此般美好不為我存在。

甜蜜的雙唇啊，我的心曾因你而破碎，

它能否躲藏好，

就不會再受到你

禁錮我那垂死的真心，

即便它只願死在你的淚水裡。

That moment from time was singled

As the first of a life of pain;

The cup of its joy was mingled

— Delusion too sweet though vain!

Too sweet to be mine again.

Sweet lips, could my heart have hidden

That its life was crushed by you,

Ye would not have then forbidden

The death which a heart so true

Sought in your briny dew.

自由頌／

自由啊，雖然你的旗幟破舊，卻依然飄揚，

有如猛烈的風暴正向狂風衝擊。

——拜倫

一支光榮的民族再度激起閃電

照耀各個國度，自由出現在

每個人心中，每座塔樓之上，席捲西班牙，

如同火焰蔓延直上雲霄，

光彩奪目。我的靈魂因而解開了陰霾的枷鎖，

乘著歌聲的翅膀，

蕭穆而強勁地飛翔，

像一隻清晨出現在雲上的雛鷹，

逆向盤旋在慣以為常的獵物上；

精神的颶風將自由包圍，流火

從遙遠的天空傳來光亮，

Ode to Liberty

Yet, Freedom, yet, thy banner, torn but flying,

Streams like a thunder-storm against the wind.

—*BYRON*

A glorious people vibrated again

The lightning of the nations: Liberty

From heart to heart, from tower to tower, o'er Spain,

Scattering contagious fire into the sky,

Gleamed. My soul spurned the chains of its dismay,

And in the rapid plumes of song

Clothed itself, sublime and strong;

As a young eagle soars the morning clouds among,

Hovering inverse o'er its accustomed prey;

Till from its station in the Heaven of fame

The Spirit's whirlwind rapped it, and the ray

Of the remotest sphere of living flame

為後方的虛空舖平道路

宛如小艇經過湍流時激起的泡沫，

當這聲音從深處發出之際：我要如實記錄。

太陽和寧靜的月亮躍出了天空，

燃燒著的群星佈滿蒼穹

猛力穿梭天庭深處。千姿百態的地表，

那座世界之洋中的一座島嶼，

在賴以維生的大氣中飄浮，

然而，在最為神聖的宇宙間，

卻是一片混沌與咒罵，

因為你不在這裡，邪惡只會產生邪惡，

只會煽動野獸般的行為，

與禽鳥與水下生物同樣低等，

他們相互鬥爭，充滿絕望，

Which paves the void was from behind it flung,

As foam from a ship's swiftness, when there came

A voice out of the deep: I will record the same.

The Sun and the serenest Moon sprang forth:

The burning stars of the abyss were hurled

Into the depths of Heaven. The daedal earth,

That island in the ocean of the world,

Hung in its cloud of all-sustaining air:

But this divinest universe

Was yet a chaos and a curse,

For thou wert not: but, power from worst producing worse,

The spirit of the beasts was kindled there,

And of the birds, and of the watery forms,

And there was war among them, and despair

怒氣不消永無止戰之際：

他們的保姆遭受玷污而

呻吟著，人、獸、蛆蟲都在互相爭鬥，

每顆心都騷動如地獄的風暴。

人類，這至高的形體，不斷繁衍後代，

在陽光的照耀下，枝繁葉茂：

居住於宮殿和金字塔，

教堂與監獄中，為數眾多，

就像狼群都住在山洞中一樣。

這數不盡的生命，

過去是野蠻、狡猾、盲目且粗暴的，

因為少了你；在人類的荒原上，

像一片烏雲俯視著海上的波濤；在下面

被尊奉著的奴隸主，是另一種邪惡；

暴虐的官吏和教徒追趕著人群，

Within them, raging without truce or terms:

The bosom of their violated nurse

Groaned, for beasts warred on beasts, and worms on worms,

And men on men; each heart was as a hell of storms.

Man, the imperial shape, then multiplied

His generations under the pavilion

Of the Sun's throne: palace and pyramid,

Temple and prison, to many a swarming million

Were, as to mountain-wolves their ragged caves.

This human living multitude

Was savage, cunning, blind, and rude,

For thou wert not; but o'er the populous solitude,

Like one fierce cloud over a waste of waves,

Hung Tyranny; beneath, sate deified

The sister-pest, congregator of slaves;

Into the shadow of her pinions wide

Anarchs and priests, who feed on gold and blood

他們僅僅貪戀鮮血和金錢，

他們的靈魂早已鏽跡斑斑。

希臘安睡的海角，湛藍的島，

起伏的波濤，似霧的山嶺，

正被光輝籠罩，接受著來自天庭的微笑：

從那靈異的岩洞中

預言的回聲傳來模糊的曲調。

在希臘無憂的原野中，

橄欖樹、穀物和野果

還是原生的，尚未為人類所用：

像海底未開的花朵，

像嬰兒腦中的思想，

像現在的事物中包含著的未來，

不朽的藝術之夢就藏在

培羅斯的山石中；詩歌就像

牙牙學語的孩子：哲學也努力地

尋找你；這時在愛琴海的平原中

Till with the stain their inmost souls are dyed,

Drove the astonished herds of men from every side.

The nodding promontories, and blue isles,

And cloud-like mountains, and dividuous waves

Of Greece, basked glorious in the open smiles

Of favouring Heaven: from their enchanted caves

Prophetic echoes flung dim melody.

On the unapprehensive wild

The vine, the corn, the olive mild,

Grew savage yet, to human use unreconciled;

And, like unfolded flowers beneath the sea,

Like the man's thought dark in the infant's brain,

Like aught that is which wraps what is to be,

Art's deathless dreams lay veiled by many a vein

Of Parian stone; and, yet a speechless child,

Verse murmured, and Philosophy did strain

Her lidless eyes for thee; when o'er the Aegean main.

雅典站了起來：就像由空中

飄揚於紫色峭壁和銀塔之上的雲霧

所構成，最偉大的工匠之作，

亦不能和它媲美：它的根基

是海底的基石，黃昏的暮色是它的帳篷；

在它的城門前，有風

在留戀，每個城池都有

雲霧的翅膀，似火的驕陽—

好一幅神聖之作！然而雅典更為聖潔，

以人的意志為拱柱，

如同鑲嵌在鑽石般的山丘上；

因為有你在，你的創新技藝

留下了永逝者的痕跡，

並在大理石上刻劃永恆，那座山

是你最早的寶座，最新的神諭。

Athens arose: a city such as vision

Builds from the purple crags and silver towers

Of battlemented cloud, as in derision

Of kingliest masonry: the ocean-floors

Pave it; the evening sky pavilions it;

Its portals are inhabited

By thunder-zoned winds, each head

Within its cloudy wings with sun-fire garlanded,—

A divine work! Athens, diviner yet,

Gleamed with its crest of columns, on the will

Of man, as on a mount of diamond, set;

For thou wert, and thine all-creative skill

Peopled, with forms that mock the eternal dead

In marble immortality, that hill

Which was thine earliest throne and latest oracle.

時光之河中還保留著雅典

碧波蕩漾的意象，一如故往

它不安地在激流中屹立，

雖然顫抖，卻不會逝去！

歌頌者和哲人的聲音宛若雷鳴，

轟隆作響震醒了大地，

響徹在往昔的山谷，

（「宗教」遮住她的雙眼；「壓迫」驚慌退縮）

那鳴聲中包含著歡樂，愛情與驚訝，

到達了「期待」從沒到過的高空，

撕破了時空的帷帳！

雲、水、露本是生於海洋；

天空被太陽照亮；一種以生命

和愛情不斷塑造著的渾濁精神，

就像雅典用光輝賦予世界新生命。

Within the surface of Time's fleeting river

Its wrinkled image lies, as then it lay

Immovably unquiet, and for ever

It trembles, but it cannot pass away!

The voices of thy bards and sages thunder

With an earth-awakening blast

Through the caverns of the past:

(Religion veils her eyes; Oppression shrinks aghast:)

A winged sound of joy, and love, and wonder,

Which soars where Expectation never flew,

Rending the veil of space and time asunder!

One ocean feeds the clouds, and streams, and dew;

One Sun illumines Heaven; one Spirit vast

With life and love makes chaos ever new,

As Athens doth the world with thy delight renew.

接著，又有了羅馬。加得穆斯女祭司

以乳房哺育幼狼，

她給予美好的乳汁；然而卻未能使幼狼

禁斷極樂園的食物；

多少恐怖的正義之舉，

因而變得聖潔；

在笑容之中，因為有你隨行，

卡蜜拉得以聖潔過活，阿蒂利亞也死得堅強。

然而，當淚水玷污你聖潔的白衣，

羅馬的宮殿受到黃金褻瀆，

你輕展精靈的雙翼，

悄悄離開了暴虐者的會議：他們已經

成為暴君的奴隸，帕拉丁

還低和著愛奧尼亞的歌曲，

但是你已經不願再聽，悲痛地與他們斷絕關係。

Then Rome was, and from thy deep bosom fairest,

Like a wolf-cub from a Cadmaean Maenad,

She drew the milk of greatness, though thy dearest

From that Elysian food was yet unweaned;

And many a deed of terrible uprightness

By thy sweet love was sanctified;

And in thy smile, and by thy side,

Saintly Camillus lived, and firm Atilius died.

But when tears stained thy robe of vestal-whiteness,

And gold profaned thy Capitolian throne,

Thou didst desert, with spirit-winged lightness,

The senate of the tyrants: they sunk prone

Slaves of one tyrant: Palatinus sighed

Faint echoes of Ionian song; that tone

Thou didst delay to hear, lamenting to disown

是從哪個赫凱尼亞的山谷或是冰川，

或從哪個北極的海岬，

或是偏僻的小島上，你是否

對頹圮王朝表示哀悼？

並交給森林、波浪和沙漠岩石，

和海中所有冰冷的岩洞

在陰鬱而悲涼的回聲中，

宣講那不被人們重視的崇高知識？

因為你不理會北歐歌者那夢中的

奇異羊群，也不再進入

朱伊德的夢中。是否你的淚水

早已風乾，你卻依然呻吟，

冷看加利利的蛇爬出死亡之海，

開始在世上燒殺擄掠，

世界頃刻間變得荒蕪。

From what Hyrcanian glen or frozen hill,

Or piny promontory of the Arctic main,

Or utmost islet inaccessible,

Didst thou lament the ruin of thy reign,

Teaching the woods and waves, and desert rocks,

And every Naiad's ice-cold urn,

To talk in echoes sad and stern

Of that sublimest lore which man had dared unlearn?

For neither didst thou watch the wizard flocks

Of the Scald's dreams, nor haunt the Druid's sleep.

What if the tears rained through thy shattered locks

Were quickly dried? for thou didst groan, not weep,

When from its sea of death, to kill and burn,

The Galilean serpent forth did creep,

And made thy world an undistinguishable heap.

千年以來，大地高呼：「你在哪裡？」

你的影子翩然而至，落在了

撒克遜阿弗瑞德纏橄欖枝的額前；

有多少聚集戰士的堡壘

像火山爆發的岩石，

在神聖的義大利崛起，

面對著國王、教士和奴隸們以威權建構的塔樓，

無視暴風雨中的大海；

無數的安那其，像泡沫般

茫然地衝擊著他們的城堡；

但從內心發出的神奇樂音，

讓這支各自為政的隊伍

感受到愛與敬畏而得以折服；不朽的藝術

又用聖杖將我們世間的住所

畫下美的形象，以建造天庭永恆的圓頂。

A thousand years the Earth cried, 'Where art thou?'

And then the shadow of thy coming fell

On Saxon Alfred's olive-cinctured brow:

And many a warrior-peopled citadel.

Like rocks which fire lifts out of the flat deep,

Arose in sacred Italy,

Frowning o'er the tempestuous sea

Of kings, and priests, and slaves, in tower-crowned majesty;

That multitudinous anarchy did sweep

And burst around their walls, like idle foam,

Whilst from the human spirit's deepest deep

Strange melody with love and awe struck dumb

Dissonant arms; and Art, which cannot die,

With divine wand traced on our earthly home

Fit imagery to pave Heaven's everlasting dome.

你是比月神還迅速的女獵者！你是

豺狼的天敵！你是弓箭的佩戴者，

就像天亮時東方的陽光灑下，雲霧就會消散，

滿載著罪惡的風暴

也能被陽光般的利劍所射穿！

路德看到你那如閃電的目光，

反射在他的鉛矛上，

融化了昏睡中的幻覺；

整個國家如同躺在那墳墓般；

英格蘭的先知稱你為女皇，

用不停歇的樂章為你雀躍歡呼，

樂聲永恆地流瀉而出；是你

走過彌爾頓的心靈之眼，

啊，目盲的詩人！他竟然能穿透

無邊的黑暗，在悲傷中看到你。

Thou huntress swifter than the Moon! thou terror

Of the world's wolves! thou bearer of the quiver,

Whose sunlike shafts pierce tempest-winged Error,

As light may pierce the clouds when they dissever

In the calm regions of the orient day!

Luther caught thy wakening glance;

Like lightning, from his leaden lance

Reflected, it dissolved the visions of the trance

In which, as in a tomb, the nations lay;

And England's prophets hailed thee as their queen,

In songs whose music cannot pass away,

Though it must flow forever: not unseen

Before the spirit-sighted countenance

Of Milton didst thou pass, from the sad scene

Beyond whose night he saw, with a dejected mien.

熱切盼望的歲歲年年，

就像站在朝霞的山巔之上，

將震耳的希望和恐懼消弭無聲，

眾人互相遮掩蒙蔽，

高喊：「自由！」穴居的憐憫

也在此時得到憤怒的呼應，

墓中的死亡被嚇得臉色發青，

禍害也在向魔鬼哀求救命！

你就像被自己的霞光所包圍的

初升旭日，

驅除每個國家中

如陰影般的的敵人，又如太陽的光輝

劃破西方海面的陰暗，

人們突然感覺到你那陌生的眼睛裡

所發出的光芒，因驚喜而甦醒。

The eager hours and unreluctant years
As on a dawn-illumined mountain stood.
Trampling to silence their loud hopes and fears,
Darkening each other with their multitude,
And cried aloud, 'Liberty!' Indignation
Answered Pity from her cave;
Death grew pale within the grave,
And Desolation howled to the destroyer, Save!
When like Heaven's Sun girt by the exhalation
Of its own glorious light, thou didst arise.
Chasing thy foes from nation unto nation
Like shadows: as if day had cloven the skies
At dreaming midnight o'er the western wave,
Men started, staggering with a glad surprise,
Under the lightnings of thine unfamiliar eyes.

人間的天堂啊！究竟是什麼魔咒能

陰險地將你遮蔽？漫長的歲月

出生在迫害的泥淖裡，

你的銀光染上了鮮血和淚水，

直到甜美的星星將污泥滌淨；

像極了酒神節的狂歡之眾

喝著嗜血之酒，率領毀滅的奴隸

戴著愚蠢之冠，包圍著法蘭西！

當時，其中一位無比強悍之人

挺身而出，這個附屬於你的化身擁有

使人困惑的力量；

投身混戰的大軍中，

像烏雲相逢，遮住了神聖的天空。

他曾受過去的迫害，

那難忘的過往已經安息，

回憶的鬼魂仍使得勝的國王驚悸！

Thou Heaven of earth! what spells could pall thee then

In ominous eclipse? a thousand years

Bred from the slime of deep Oppression's den.

Dyed all thy liquid light with blood and tears.

Till thy sweet stars could weep the stain away;

How like Bacchanals of blood

Round France, the ghastly vintage, stood

Destruction's sceptred slaves, and Folly's mitred brood!

When one, like them, but mightier far than they,

The Anarch of thine own bewildered powers,

Rose: armies mingled in obscure array,

Like clouds with clouds, darkening the sacred bowers

Of serene Heaven. He, by the past pursued,

Rests with those dead, but unforgotten hours,

Whose ghosts scare victor kings in their ancestral towers.

英國還在沉睡：難道她沒有被喚醒？

西班牙對她呼喊，伊特納

已經被維蘇威的雷聲喚醒，

那積雪的山岩已被回應聲劈為兩半。

從彼色久莎到彼羅拉，每座

希臘的海島都在波光中

閃耀、呼喊和歡跳：

天堂的燈光熄滅吧，我們不再需要你的光照！

希臘的枷鎖是條金線，只要一笑

就會消融；而西班牙的枷鎖

則是鋼條，只能藉由美德這把銼刀使力。

命運雷同的雙胞胎啊！請向

遙遠的西方，那寶座上的永恆求救；

請把你們的所思所做，

印在我們心上！時間無法加以隱蔽。

England yet sleeps: was she not called of old?

Spain calls her now, as with its thrilling thunder

Vesuvius wakens Aetna, and the cold

Snow-crags by its reply are cloven in sunder:

O'er the lit waves every Aeolian isle

From Pithecusa to Pelorus

Howls, and leaps, and glares in chorus:

They cry, 'Be dim; ye lamps of Heaven suspended o'er us!'

Her chains are threads of gold, she need but smile

And they dissolve; but Spain's were links of steel,

Till bit to dust by virtue's keenest file.

Twins of a single destiny! appeal

To the eternal years enthroned before us

In the dim West; impress us from a seal,

All ye have thought and done! Time cannot dare conceal.

阿敏納斯的墳墓啊！請交出死者！

讓他的靈魂如同哨樓上舞動的旗幟，

在暴君的頭頂上迎風飄揚，

你的勝利才是他的墓誌銘！

狂飲真理神秘瓊漿的狂徒，

日耳曼受到君主欺騙，

他死去的靈魂住在你的軀體。

為什麼我們要害怕或希冀？你已經獲得了自由！

你啊，這聖潔的天堂！

榮耀的世界！鮮花盛開的原野！

永恆的島嶼！你是祭壇，

荒蕪披著美好的衣裳，

向昨日之你頂禮膜拜！噢，義大利，

凝聚心中的熱血；鎮壓那群

以你神聖的宮廷作為巢穴的野獸吧！

Tomb of Arminius! render up thy dead

Till, like a standard from a watch-tower's staff,

His soul may stream over the tyrant's head;

Thy victory shall be his epitaph,

Wild Bacchanal of truth's mysterious wine,

King-deluded Germany,

His dead spirit lives in thee.

Why do we fear or hope? thou art already free!

And thou, lost Paradise of this divine

And glorious world! thou flowery wilderness!

Thou island of eternity! thou shrine

Where Desolation, clothed with loveliness,

Worships the thing thou wert! O Italy,

Gather thy blood into thy heart; repress

The beasts who make their dens thy sacred palaces.

希望自由之人能將「帝王」這褻瀆的名諱

視為塵土！要不就將它寫在土裡，

讓榮譽的頁面沾上污漬，

就像被風抹去的蛇蠍足跡，

被沙土所覆蓋！

你們已聽到這個預言：

請高舉你那榮耀的勝利之劍，

把污濁的哥帝爾斯的愁結斬斷！

它雖已如殘梗般微弱，卻還能

把震懾的棍棒和斧頭

牢固地捆在一起，讓人類感到恐懼；

這字音中有一種毒素，能讓生活腐朽、邪惡、難以忍受；

你不該驕傲自大，在那命定的時刻，

用你全副武裝的腳後跟

踐踏這該死卻不甘的蛆蟲。

Oh, that the free would stamp the impious name

Of KING into the dust! or write it there,

So that this blot upon the page of fame

Were as a serpent's path, which the light air

Erases, and the flat sands close behind!

Ye the oracle have heard:

Lift the victory-flashing sword.

And cut the snaky knots of this foul gordian word,

Which, weak itself as stubble, yet can bind

Into a mass, irrefragably firm,

The axes and the rods which awe mankind;

The sound has poison in it, 'tis the sperm

Of what makes life foul, cankerous, and abhorred;

Disdain not thou, at thine appointed term,

To set thine armed heel on this reluctant worm.

希望智者可以用他們的智慧

照亮世間的幽暗，

讓「教徒」這個蒼白的稱謂，

躲到地獄去：這才是它的處所，──

它是魔鬼褻瀆神靈時發出的嘲笑聲；

但願人類的思想，

只膜拜理性，

這才是主宰他的無畏靈魂，

所尊奉的寶座！無窮的力量！

思想模糊的文字，

就像明淨湖水中晶亮的露珠形成的雲霧

有時會遮掩天庭的藍天，

但願有朝能剝去那層薄紗和一切

非屬自身的色調、愁容和微笑。

直到虛假與真實都得以赤裸本色

面對天空，適得其所！

Oh, that the wise from their bright minds would kindle

Such lamps within the dome of this dim world,

That the pale name of PRIEST might shrink and dwindle

Into the hell from which it first was hurled,

A scoff of impious pride from fiends impure;

Till human thoughts might kneel alone,

Each before the judgement-throne

Of its own aweless soul, or of the Power unknown!

Oh, that the words which make the thoughts obscure

From which they spring, as clouds of glimmering dew

From a white lake blot Heaven's blue portraiture,

Were stripped of their thin masks and various hue

And frowns and smiles and splendours not their own,

Till in the nakedness of false and true

They stand before their Lord, each to receive its due!

如果有人曾教人類去征服

一切妨礙生命進程的事物，

將自己奉為生命的主人。噢，那都是徒勞無功！

若是人自己心甘情願為奴，

仍視壓制與壓迫者為主人，

即便大地能讓人們衣食無憂，

以豐沛的資源滿足人類欲求，

那權利不就如同種子孕育著樹木，只存在思想裡？

即便是藝術這位熱心的和解者，

振動著火焰般的羽翼，飛到自然的寶座前，

讓大地母親停止對她的愛撫，

喊道：「把你對天地的掌控權給我吧」又會如何？

若生活總是衍生出

新的匱乏，勞苦呻吟者的所有、

你我得自上天的饋贈，將被千百倍剝奪，

只為給一人任意揮霍！

He who taught man to vanquish whatsoever

Can be between the cradle and the grave

Crowned him the King of Life. Oh, vain endeavour!

If on his own high will, a willing slave,

He has enthroned the oppression and the oppressor

What if earth can clothe and feed

Amplest millions at their need,

And power in thought be as the tree within the seed?

Or what if Art, an ardent intercessor,

Driving on fiery wings to Nature's throne,

Checks the great mother stooping to caress her,

And cries: 'Give me, thy child, dominion

Over all height and depth'?

if Life can breed

New wants, and wealth from those who toil and groan,

Rend of thy gifts and hers a thousandfold for one!

來吧，請同時將來自人類精神最深處的

智慧帶來，就像晨星

將太陽從伊奧的海面上喚醒。

聽啊，智慧女神的馬車正在前進，

像是彩雲被火焰驅動；

永恆思想的統治者啊，

你難道不想和她同來，

用真理來評判不公允的命運，

盲目的愛、裁判公正、

過去的榮譽以及未來的希望？

自由啊！如果這能稱為你的名字，

你和這所有的一切怎能解脫？

如果你和他們的珍寶可以用

鮮血和淚水交換，難道那些智者和自由的人們

不是已流出眼淚，和淚一般的血嗎？莊嚴的歌聲—

Come thou, but lead out of the inmost cave

Of man's deep spirit, as the morning-star

Beckons the Sun from the Eoan wave,

Wisdom. I hear the pennons of her car

Self-moving, like cloud charioted by flame;

Comes she not, and come ye not,

Rulers of eternal thought,

To judge, with solemn truth, life's ill-apportioned lot?

Blind Love, and equal Justice, and the Fame

Of what has been, the Hope of what will be?

O Liberty! if such could be thy name

Wert thou disjoined from these, or they from thee:

If thine or theirs were treasures to be bought

By blood or tears, have not the wise and free

Wept tears, and blood like tears?—The solemn harmony

到此停歇：歌唱的精靈

突然變得沉默，回到了它的深淵：

像雲雀莊嚴地飛進清晨的

霧中，突遭雷電，

在金光照耀下從空中墜落，

僵直地落在沉默的平原中；

又像一支遙遠的燭光，

消逝在黑夜；像夏日的雲朵

在天上灑盡雨水，然後隱退；

像短命的蜉蝣與白晝一同逝去，

我的歌聲因失去了神奇的翅膀

而停歇，連曾支撐它飛翔的的偉大回聲

也已在遠方消失，

就像剛鋪路的海中波浪，

又在波濤洶湧中淹沒溺水者的頭顱，嘶嘶作響。

Paused, and the Spirit of that mighty singing

To its abyss was suddenly withdrawn;

Then, as a wild swan, when sublimely winging

Its path athwart the thunder-smoke of dawn,

Sinks headlong through the aereal golden light

On the heavy-sounding plain,

When the bolt has pierced its brain;

As summer clouds dissolve, unburthened of their rain;

As a far taper fades with fading night,

As a brief insect dies with dying day,

My song, its pinions disarrayed of might,

Drooped; o'er it closed the echoes far away

Of the great voice which did its flight sustain,

As waves which lately paved his watery way

Hiss round a drowner's head in their tempestuous play.

關於作者 ————

　　珀西・比希・雪萊（Percy Bysshe Shelley，1792—1822），是英國浪漫主義後期著名的抒情詩人，也是歷史上最出色的英語詩人之一。他出生在英格蘭一個貴族家庭。從小聰穎，8歲就寫了第一首詩《貓》。在伊頓公學就讀期間，他深受英國著名啟蒙思想家威廉・葛德文的《政治正義論》的影響。在牛津大學就讀不到半年，他就因寫作了《無神論的必然》而被開除。不久，他因娶了一位平民女子而被父親逐出家門，成為英國上流社會的逐客。

　　雪萊具有激進的民主思想，積極參與愛爾蘭反對英國殖民統治的鬥爭。他寫於1813年的第一部長詩《麥布女王》和1818年的《伊斯蘭的起義》等作品更是激怒了英國的上流社會。因此，藉由他的婚姻問題，上流社會對雪萊發動了無休止的責難和迫害，迫使他憤然離開祖國，寄居義大利。在最後的歲月裡，詩人寫下了詩劇《解放的普羅米修斯》等一系列不朽之作。

　　1822年，雪萊泛舟出海，因覆舟被巨浪吞噬，年輕的生命，就此劃下句點。

　　本書精選了雪萊眾多詩篇中的代表作，其中包括為人熟知的《致雲雀》、《西風頌》，充滿戰鬥激情的《愛爾蘭人之歌》，優美而深情的《音樂》……，每一首詩無不令人回味吟詠。書中精選的這些詩，反映了雪萊詩歌的獨特風格：清新、真摯，充滿了對大自然的美與崇高精神的深情讚頌，以及對當時專制、黑暗社會的無比憎恨以及對人類社會光明前景的預言。

　　《西風頌》謳歌了秋風摧枯拉朽、蕩滌一切污穢腐敗的磅礴氣勢，及其詛咒嚴冬，呼喚生機盎然、大好春光的激情。它是雪萊的代表作，也是讚詠自由理想、嚮往美好生活和大無畏奮鬥精神的不朽頌歌。

1792	0	8 月 4 日，雪萊生於英國薩塞克斯郡霍舍姆附近的菲爾德·普·萊斯之世代貴族家庭中。為家中長子，共有四個妹妹及一個弟弟。
1800	8	開始嘗試創作，詩作為《貓》。
1802	10	入薩昂學校（Sion House Academy）就讀。
1804	12	入伊頓公學（Eton College）。雪萊在校近六年，備受貴族子弟同輩欺壓；但雪萊學業優良，尤其拉丁詩出色超群。雪萊在伊頓除研讀葛德文著作外，亦讀盧克萊修（Lucretius），普里尼(Pliny)…等著作，也大量研讀自然科學書籍。
1810	18	於 10 月入學牛津大學。同年 4 月尚在伊頓時，已出版與妹妹合著之小說《扎斯特洛齊》(Zastrozzi)。9 月出版《維克多和卡齊爾詩集》。入學牛津後，於 11 月出版《瑪格雷特·尼柯爾遜遺篇》，12 月出版《聖·伊爾文》均顯露出反封建思想。
1811	19	3 月 25 日因刊行《無神論的必然》一文遭牛津大學開除，於 3 月 26 日離校。8 月 28 日與妹妹的同學哈麗特·威斯布魯克結婚。婚後住在凱斯維克（Keswick），得知葛德文仍健在。同年與黑奇納女士（Miss Hitchner）通信，大多談論哲學、政治等相關議題。

1812	20	1月與葛德文通信。2月12日～4月4日赴愛爾蘭進行政治活動，在都柏林刊行《告愛爾蘭人民書》、《成立博愛主義者協會倡議書》、《人權宣言》等文件，並在都柏林集會上發表演講，談天主教徒解放等問題。6～8月住林茂斯（Lynmouth），刊行《效艾棱巴羅勛爵的信》。著手寫作《麥布女王》敘事長詩。10月於倫敦會見葛德文。
1813	21	於2月完成《麥布女王》敘事長詩及散文註釋（無法公開出版）。再次訪問愛爾蘭。
1814	22	7月與哈麗特·威斯布魯克離異，而開始與葛德文之女瑪麗·吳爾史東克拉芙特·葛德文同居。出版《駁自然種論》一書。
1815	23	1月祖父逝世。按照當時的長子繼承法，當時在經濟上十分拮据的雪萊獲得了一筆遺產，但他並未獨佔，而是與妹妹分享。8月定居溫莎附近的比曉普蓋特（Bishopgate）。創作《阿拉斯特》、《一個共和主義者有感於波拿巴的垮台》、《致華茲渥斯》等詩。這些詩，連同《阿拉斯特》長詩，均於1816年出版。
1816	24	3月，刊行《阿拉斯特》等詩。5月～9月間旅行瑞士日內瓦一帶，開始與拜倫交往密切。12月10日，前妻哈麗特投河自盡。之後遂與瑪麗·吳爾史東克拉芙特正式結婚。開始與自由主義者李希·亨特（Leigh Hunt）等人往來。

1817	25	2月5日，與詩人濟慈（John Keats）相識。法庭判處剝奪雪萊與前妻所生子女之撫養權。遂作《致大法官》一詩，表示抗議。創作長詩《伊斯蘭的反叛》。發表《關於在整個王國實行選舉制度改革的建議》、《為夏洛蒂公主去世告人民書》等手冊。
1818	26	出版《伊斯蘭的起義》。於4月抵達義大利，從此便未返回英國。撰寫巨著《解放的普羅米修斯》第一幕，11月走訪羅馬和龐貝，之後定居於那不勒斯。
1819	27	完成《解放的普羅米修斯》全詩劇四幕。完成詩劇《倩契》。作政論《從哲學的觀點看議會改革》但並未完稿。發生曼徹斯特群眾集會遭到騎兵屠殺事件，雪萊對此極為憤慨，開始創作政治長詩《暴政的假面遊行》及其他詩篇。代表作《西風頌》亦於此年創作完成。
1820	28	《解放的普羅米修斯及其他》詩集出版。完成《阿特拉斯的女巫》一詩。創作《自由頌》長詩，該詩顯露了歷史唯物主義的萌芽。
1821	29	2月濟慈逝世。雪萊即作長詩《阿多尼》以示悼念。著作《為詩辯護》，回應友人皮柯克的詩論。撰寫最後巨著抒情詩劇《希臘》，讚頌希臘人民在土耳其暴君統治下爭取自由。

| 1822 | 30 | 抒情詩劇《希臘》出版。6 月創作長詩《生命的凱旋》，並未完成。7 月 8 日於返家途中，斯貝齊亞海上驟起風暴，雪萊及同船兩人皆因覆舟被巨浪吞噬，生命於此劃下句點。 |

國家圖書館出版品預行編目(CIP)資料

雪萊詩選：西風頌 / 雪萊著；王明鳳譯.
-- 初版. -- 臺北市：笛藤, 2018.05
　　面；　公分. --（世界經典文學）
中英對照雙語版
ISBN 978-957-710-718-3（平裝）
873.51　　　　　　　　　107003010

2018年5月23日　初版第1刷　定價300元

雪萊詩選 / 西風頌
中英對照雙語版

著　　　者	雪萊
譯　　　者	王明鳳
審　　　譯	陳珮馨
封面設計	王舒玕
內頁設計	王舒玕
總　編　輯	賴巧凌
發　行　所	笛藤出版圖書有限公司
發　行　人	林建仲
地　　　址	台北市中山區長安東路二段171號3樓3室
電　　　話	(02)2777-3682
傳　　　真	(02)2777-3672
總　經　銷	聯合發行股份有限公司
地　　　址	新北市新店區寶橋路235巷6弄6號2樓
電　　　話	(02)2917-8022・(02)2917-8042
製　版　廠	造極彩色印刷製版股份有限公司
地　　　址	新北市中和區中山路2段340巷36號
電　　　話	(02)2240-0333・(02)2248-3904
劃撥帳戶	八方出版股份有限公司
劃撥帳號	19809050